The Double-Sided Man

Third Novel of the Spy Wars Trilogy

The Double-Sided Man

Donald J. Farinacci

NAVIGATOR BOOKS

SAN DIEGO, CALIFORNIA

THE DOUBLE-SIDED MAN

Copyright © 2016 by Donald J. Farinacci

Cover design by Tom Heffron.

Navigator Books

www.navigator-books.com

ISBN-13: 978-1-940397-93-1

Printed in the United States of America

The Spy Wars Trilogy

The Allemagne Deception (2011)

1961-Sliding Toward Armageddon (2012)

The Double-Sided Man (2016)

*"Oh what a tangled web
we weave when first
we practice to deceive."*

—Sir Walter Scott

Foreword

The Double-Sided Man is a suspenseful and unique thriller rooted in the war against Islamic Jihad – a realistic spy novel for the thinking individual.

Staying true to the use of classic espionage trade-craft, a small CIA team of men and women stand toe to toe with America's enemies – both foreign and domestic – in defense of the homeland.

It is a story of the travails of the modern world, yet has its genesis in the intrigue of World War II and the Cold War. It was during that span of time that intricate espionage techniques such as the "double-cross" were employed to the maximum.

Interwoven with this tale of physical and intellectual warfare in an age of terrorism are gripping personal dramas of siblings, parents, children, husbands and wives enmeshed within the forces of history and fate, over which they have little control.

Though decades have passed since the WWII–Cold War era, the most diabolical and malevolent operatives of that time are back – reincarnate in their natural descendants. A new war is in progress, testing not only the courage and resourcefulness of the American combatants but also those core values which define what it means to a responsible citizen of a democracy.

CONTENTS

Chapter One

BOOKER

Richmond Tallifierro (pronounced "Tollifer") disliked taking a seat on public conveyances. His penchant for standing erect on busses, subways and commuter trains stemmed from a mixture of impatience and curiosity. He was impatient to get where he was going and curious about those sharing the ride.

Sitting down he could view and study only a few fellow passengers. But at a height of six feet, three inches, standing up afforded him an overview of all of them.

Being conspicuous as he towered over most others on the train, trolley or bus had never been a professional disadvantage, given that Richmond (nicknamed Rick) had been non-operational for his short career. Analysts like him were fungible goods in most national intelligence services; at least that's what he thought.

Even Rick's closest friends were ignorant of the character traits from which his oddly habitual behavior sprang. And as the Metro subway noisily plodded from the Washington Monument towards the Capitol and the U.S. Supreme Court at the opposite end of the

Mall, Rick mused that while everyone he knew as more than an acquaintance was aware of his unswerving devotion to remaining vertical on short trips, no other person—not even Clarissa—knew the reasons why. Were the reasons important? Probably only to him.

By turns, this thought led him to ruminate on just how difficult it was to really know another person, to grasp the inherently deep mysteries of the other's inner-self, and the acquired traits engrafted upon one's soul. For that matter, although he had shared bed and board with Clarissa for four years, how well did he really know her deepest self?

Yes, he knew her likes and dislikes, her preferences in books, music, food, wine, art, politics and men. But, did he truly know her darkest desires, her most strongly-held convictions and her deepest fears? And what of the unconscious mind, that receptacle for all of the accumulated frustrations, hurts, slights, traumas and shameful regrets resident in one's psyche?

Clarissa wasn't a big talker about herself but even if she were, just how reliable are the verbalizings of introspection and feelings? The inner streams of one's nature are seldom revealed by most expressions of emotion or thought.

Rick knew with an unassailable certainty that most people had a well-hidden self because he himself had one; and that's what drew him to espionage in the first place—an attraction he shared with his father, Tom Tallifierro, former analyst extraordinaire for several U.S. intelligence agencies.

From his vantage point, Rick spied two middle-aged men seated at the far end of the car, engaged in earnest conversation. They were essentially nondescript, except for the concerned expressions they wore. Did he catch the stocky one toss a quick and furtive glance his way? He thought so. Both men were Caucasians of average height, one thin and the other portly. Neither of them wore a suit or tie. The less bulky of the two wore blue jeans, a zippered sweat jacket and athletic shoes; the other, khaki pants, a forest-green windbreaker and brown loafers. They warranted Rick's further attention.

Keeping one eye on the two men, Rick let his mind wander to his upcoming schedule for the day. At 10:00 a.m., he would meet on Capitol Hill with Representative Mark Scherzer of Utah, the Chairman of the House Armed Services Committee. He had been tasked by the CIA, commonly referred to as the Company, with the job of fully briefing the Congressman on the recent and frantic spate of actions taken by Russia to refurbish its nuclear arsenal, in reaction to the U.S. program of nuclear modernization agreed upon between President Obama and Congress. It was not a task he looked forward to. The prickly and starkly ambitious Scherzer was, in Rick's judgment, unreliable and indiscreet. Before each briefing Rick would emphasize and re-emphasize that the session was classified and highly confidential. Scherzer would wholeheartedly agree to keep it secret. Then, the more headline-worthy information would be leaked to the media by "informed sources."

Rick got off the Metro at the Capitol Hill exit. The two men followed him. He wondered if they were "watchers," in counterintelligence parlance. He'd know soon. It wasn't difficult for a man with Rick's training to spot a tail, or to lose one. As he climbed the steps of the Capitol building, the two men remained on the sidewalk below, smoking and engaging in feigned conversation.

Rick was greeted in the Congressman's waiting room by Kyle Collins, Scherzer's Administrative Assistant and enforcer-in-chief. The meeting with Scherzer was not unlike the other half-dozen or so they had had in the past. Rick conducted the briefing in a conversational tone while Scherzer interrupted frequently to take and make phone calls, issue commands on his intercom, ask agenda-driven questions to Rick, glance at memos placed in front of him by staffers, and, at intervals, get up from his desk and leave the room. No explanation or excuse was offered either when he left or returned. After 40 minutes to the second, Collins opened the door and signaled to Scherzer with a quick tomahawk chop that the meeting was over. Scherzer got up and left.

Rick drank deeply at the water cooler in the corridor afterwards, as if to wash away the bad taste in his mouth. He hoped his next meeting with Douglas Booker, the retiring head of the CIA would be more productive. Doug Booker was both Rick's boss and a long-time friend of the Tallifierro family. Booker was especially close to Tom Tallifierro with whom he had served in U.S. Army Intelligence from 1967 through 1969. They had joined forces in '68 in breaking the Soviet Union's vaunted "Allemagne Deception," in Germany and Czechoslovakia. With the help of their colleagues they had probably prevented World War III, thereby gaining legendary status for themselves within the cloistered corridors of Western Intelligence agencies.

A steady drizzle fell on Rick's bare head and on those of his watchers as he reached the bottom of the Capitol steps and turned in the direction of the Underground entrance. The late October dampness and chill only added to the melancholy which had engulfed him the last few weeks. The reasons were varied. First there was the death of retired General Frederick Reitenhauser at the age of 89, from what was claimed to be congestive heart failure. Reitenhauser had also been a steadfast family friend since Tom Tallifierro served as lead analyst for the Army's 409th Special Investigations Detachment. Reitenhauser was his commanding officer. This all happened in 1968 and 1969 in Munich, West Germany, at the height of the Cold War. When Tom's genius not only averted a hot war but saved Reitenhauser's career, a bond was formed between the two men which lasted for the remainder of the former general's life. To Rick, Reitenhauser had been more like a kindly uncle than a family friend. Without Reitenhauser's encouragement and guidance, it is unlikely Rick would have chosen intelligence work as a career.

Reitenhauser retired from the Army in 1985 to become Director of the CIA (DCI). In 1995 with the onset of old age approaching he left the CIA and named Doug Booker as his handpicked successor. Now Booker was retiring too. One by one, the heroes of Rick's youth were passing from the scene.

Rick himself was now thirty-seven and had been a senior analyst for six years without a promotion or increase in pay grade. During that same six-year period, Clarissa, two years his junior, had gone from the position of an associate in the litigation department of the Wall Street law firm, Thurman, Bixby and Reed, to a trial partner, with aggregate annual raises over the time period totaling $125,000.00. Of course, he was happy for her, but the disparity in their career advancements filled him right now with only gloom.

The gray sky hung over Washington like a harbinger of doom. Rick decided to break his dim mood by losing the tail. He walked quickly to the entrance of the Underground and descended the stairs. The two watchers were about thirty yards behind him. Before they had time to reach the bottom of the stairs, he had sprinted to the exit on the opposite side of the station, took the stairs three at a time up to the street and walked swiftly parallel to the Mall, until he reached Union Station. There he grabbed a taxi, slid down in the back seat and ordered the driver to take him on the double to his hotel, the Hay-Adams, bordering on Lafayette Park behind the White House. From his hotel room he could see Secret Service sharpshooters on the roof of the White House.

In his room, Rick made himself a cup of coffee and called down to Valet Parking to have his car brought to the front entrance of the hotel. From there he would embark on the second leg of his trip. He would drive to the other side of the Potomac and head for CIA Headquarters in Langley, Virginia, through suburban Northern Virginia. The drive to Langley from downtown DC usually took about 40 minutes to an hour. Rick made it to the outer gates in 35 minutes. He drove a 2014, fully-loaded, Lexus LS. Rick didn't believe in sparing himself any of the luxuries in automobiles. He also didn't worry about speeding tickets. He acquired many each year, all of them quashed by the CIA Director's Office. The words "for reasons of national security" had a broad reach.

As he drove, congratulating himself prematurely for ditching the tail back at the Capitol, Rick took careful note of a gray Ford Falcon parked at the side of the road, perhaps two hundred meters from the front gates of the CIA. He slowed down as he passed to get a good look at the occupants and snapped their picture with his smart phone as he drove by. Two men were seated in the front seat. They were wearing the same clothes they wore on the subway, except that now each of them had on a baseball cap: one emblazoned with the name and logo of the Washington Redskins; the other with "George Washington U" on the front. Both men looked down as Rick passed by, but there was no doubt that they were the same men who had tailed him from the subway earlier that day.

Rick's counter-surveillance skills left him with no reservations as to their identities. For a few brief seconds he entertained the idea of turning around and confronting them as to who they were and why they were tailing him. But he was already late for his appointment and, actually, they hadn't tailed him to Langley. He clearly lost them back in DC. That fact was more disturbing than the tail. Somehow, they knew in advance of his appointment at Langley. They also knew ahead of time that he had business earlier at Congress.

He had walked earlier that day from the Hay-Adams to the Metro Station near the Washington Monument, and by the use of his best counter-surveillance techniques, had satisfied himself that he had no company for his first walk that day.

At Langley, Rick produced his photo I.D. at the gate to the uniformed guard and was waved on through after the guard made sure his appointment with the DCI had been logged into the computer. The guard provided him with a credential to wear around his neck.

As he rode the elevator to the fifth floor, Rick's mind was besieged with questions. How could the watchers have possibly known his schedule for the day? Equally perplexing was why they would be making such an effort to track a mid-level analyst? He knew what would be item number one on the agenda of his meeting with DCI Booker.

Always affable but reserved, Douglas Booker greeted Tallifierro with a formal hand shake; but Rick thought he caught a look of welcoming affection flicker across the older man's face.

Booker's office was spacious but the furniture was essentially functional. His desk was an unprepossessing, but solid mahogany with an aircraft carrier-style top. It did not surprise Rick in the least that Booker would want to maximize his working space. A non-ostentatious coffee table occupied the center of Booker's office, surrounded by a plain government-issue couch and several upholstered chairs. Booker sat down in one of the chairs while he gestured to Rick to sit on the couch on the opposite side of the coffee table.

The Doug Booker who fixed Rick with his penetrating gaze across the coffee table was, in essence, the same man his father first met in 1967. But that was the invisible Booker. What became visible was the result of a complete metamorphosis in the last 45 years.

Rick grew up hearing stories about the young Doug Booker, the brilliant spy and counterspy, the peerless espionage planner and analyst. He of the unkempt appearance: disheveled, rumpled and indifferent to grooming, but with a razor-sharp, penetrating mind, that even within the rigid discipline of the military, allowed him to smash to pieces the half-baked notions of his superiors. He did so with impunity, even to the brink of insubordination. When Rick's father and the other old boys from Munich got together to tell war stories, the most frequently-heard refrain was, "Only Doug Booker could have gotten away with that."

Now, however, though the probing and penetrating intellect was still as incisive as ever, the unkempt and eccentric iconoclast was long gone.

Booker was now a polished intelligence officer who carried an air of command about him. He dressed neatly with a subdued stylishness, and spoke softly but with great confidence. He displayed none of his youthful arrogance and irreverence. He was now unerringly polite. No traces of his earlier eccentricity were visible.

How was it possible for a man to undergo such a radical transformation of personality and demeanor? The answer to that intriguing question probably lay in the nature of the life of an espionage man. In the multi-layered world of secrecy, deception, hidden agendas and elaborate cover personas, any kind of bizarre behavior patterns were usually maladaptive to the successful performance of the job. Controversial behavior drew attention; and attracting attention was mutually exclusive with being an effective spymaster or agent handler.

As the years went by, the reputation of Douglas Booker as an intelligence genius steadily grew. But the greater his renown, the more reclusive he became, until now he was a practically invisible legend. He almost never was seen or heard in public.

At the age of 79, Booker was the combination of a skilled inside politician, superb intelligence operative and man of practical wisdom. But, although others did not, Booker saw himself as slightly past his prime. It was time, he reluctantly concluded, to step aside. In a little more than three months, he would leave Langley for good and retire to private life.

As Rick returned Booker's gaze, he pondered twin mysteries. Why had he attracted a tail? And equally important, why had he, a mid-level analyst with neither field nor administrative experience, been summoned here in the first place to meet with, arguably, the top intelligence man in the world?

"I had lunch with your father the other day, Richmond."

"Wait, let me guess. At the Hoyas in Georgetown."

"I didn't realize we had gotten so predictable in our old age."

"I can only speak of my father. Since he retired from Georgetown U., he has lunched at The Hoyas at least once a week. All of us in the Tallifierro family think that it's his way of putting off having to cut the cord completely."

"Ah yes, I understand. As brilliant an analyst as Tom was back in the 60s, he could never seem to break the habit of establishing predictable patterns of behavior, a fatal shortcoming in an intelligence operative. That's why Reitenhauser and I decided to keep him out of the field. And had he not had the quiet sanctuary of the Company's headquarters to unravel KGB plots, one can only guess where we'd be today. So we made Berger operational instead. He was far more suited to it. It's hard to imagine two closer friends, who were more dissimilar, than Ben Berger and your dad."

"Ben Berger, that's a name I haven't heard in a long time."

"Really? I thought Ben and Tom remained close friends over the decades."

"They did but something happened about ten years ago. I don't know what it was."

Rick hesitated in answering because intuitively he sensed that Booker already knew far more about Berger than he; and already knew the answer to the question.

"Retired from the FBI, but still doing consulting work for them, as far as I know."

Booker had either decided that enough small talk had passed between them; or he had elicited what he wanted to know and it was time to move on to the reasons for which he had summoned Rick to his office. He smoothly changed the subject.

It was not Booker's way to provide any kind of a preamble before introducing a serious subject and he made no exception now. "Richmond, as you can imagine we have had our hands full with both the ISIS situation in Iraq and Syria, and Putin's machinations in the eastern Ukraine. Stacked on top of that, our agents on the ground in Ukraine tell us that pro-Soviet militias acting as Putin's surrogates, have built up a huge cache of state-of-the-art nuclear and biological weapons not too far from the site of the crash of the Dutch airliner. Our deep-cover people in Kiev have reported that the arms depot was the real reason the pro-Soviet guerrillas stalled and delayed in providing access to the crash site, to both official investigators and the media. Until they could secure and hide the site, they were afraid that some U.N. investigator or enterprising reporter would stumble upon the site, which was supposed to be top secret. It's a sore subject at the Defense Department because the cognoscenti there know that both the U.S. and Russia would now be proceeding toward a new nuclear arms reduction treaty had Congress not forced Obama's hand by pressuring him to agree to modernize our nuclear arsenal in return for funding the arms reduction efforts called for by the treaty. Instead of facilitating mutual arms reduction, the world now has nuclear escalation and proliferation. There is little doubt that Russia only built up its Ukrainian stock piles to maintain the balance of power between them and us."

"It's starting to look more and more like a new cold war out there. And just like in the 50s, I don't see our side winning at this point. Russia's intervention in Syria is a case in point."

"Do you mind telling me why you think that?"

"No, I don't mind at all. For reasons which will become clear in a little while, it is important that you be brought fully up to speed. We have a fair amount to cover so how about a cup of coffee or tea?"

A surge of excitement coursed through Rick like an electric shock. What was happening here? Was he actually being rescued from the wasteland of ten-hour days reading Russian cables to and from their U.N. Consulate and transcripts of bugged conversations in Jersey City mosques? Douglas Booker wanted to bring him up to speed. Why him? But he'd have to hold that thought till later.

"Sure, coffee black would be great," Rick replied, trying not to betray his excitement.

With his usual air of quiet authority, Booker placed the order, which included an English breakfast tea for himself, over his intercom.

Although Rick was stationed in Manhattan for the time being, the Washington scene was in his blood. The sight of the Washington Monument in the distance from his hotel room window brought Rick a combined sense of happiness, serenity and patriotic fervor.

Sensing Rick's elevated mood, Booker took the opportunity to exploit it: "Rick, the old guard is passing and we need new blood in leading our battle against both a newly-aggressive Kremlin and a newly-resurgent Jihad." Rick offered no comment. Booker had to make his play at this own pace and in his own way. Like a master symphony conductor, he would not compromise his presentation until each magnificent movement had risen to its crescendo and was carried to a stirring finale.

Booker continued: "It's not as though we have spared any effort or resource in our intelligence efforts. From the very first classified report we received concerning escalated KGB and GRU (Russian military intelligence) activity in the Crimea, we shifted from business as usual to maximum overdrive. Every station chief and case officer from the Baltics to Ankara, and from there to Sevastopol, were put on alert and tasked with recruiting new agents, and redirecting old ones into the Crimea and eastern Ukraine, there to infiltrate; set up new networks; trawl for leads; recruit new spies, and get us the info on just what Putin and his boys are up to in that part of the world. We recruited and trained spies, agent handlers, eavesdropping experts, cyber technicians, cryptographers, code breakers, linguists, drone operators and polygraph examiners."

"No expense was spared. We were also getting at the same time signals from Yemen, Iraq, Tunisia and other places that an incipient Islamic State with an army to back it up was being molded in Eastern Syria. Our friends in the Kurdish region of Iraq were particularly alarmed. We figured that it was impossible, in the face of a double or triple international threat, to add too many additional personnel. ISIS, an acronym for Islamic State in Iraq and Syria, was galvanizing its disparate groups to organize a formidable army. We figured our greatly enhanced intelligence army would not go to waste. And it hasn't, in a manner of speaking, that is. But this is where the story gets interesting."

Rick's studied attempt at nonchalance was not lost on Booker; nor was Booker concerned about it. The old spymaster had the same effect on almost everyone. He knew Tallifierro's calm demeanor was feigned, and considered it the first telltale sign that his old magic was working.

Booker took a sip of tea, savored it and continued his monologue.

"It is difficult at this stage to point to the moment when I first realized that our enemies' recent aggressions against us were connected and coordinated. Everything—the hackers' cyberattack on J. P. Morgan/Chase's digital networks, WikiLeaks's public disclosure of government secrets, the terrorist attack by Eastern European—linked Islamic radicals at the Boston Marathon, lone-wolf jihadists on U.S. soil, the attacks by ISIS on regions occupied by U.S. allies, Putin's land-grab via annexation of the Crimea and his flagrant effort to assimilate the eastern Ukraine into Russia. It was all part of a common scheme. A plan of warfare, not necessarily involving American armies, rather a more multifaceted and insidious form of warfare. My full awareness of the scope of the offensive came only gradually, admittedly with some denial delaying my grasp of the truth."

"But by early Spring we began hitting back hard. The NSA's interception of our enemies' communications was enhanced tenfold. We quickly and dramatically increased both our technological and human intelligence resources. We infiltrated spy teams and insurgents into eastern Ukraine, the Crimea, Georgia, the Caucasus, Chechnya, Kazakhstan, Tajikistan; and inside Russia's border—from the Baltic Sea to the Black Sea. We were also successful in penetrating and planting moles in Al Qaeda, ISIS and the Shiite-controlled government of Iran. Our case officers in the Middle East, Europe, and Africa were spread thin, but we launched a crash program to send in fresh blood. We doubled several of their agents, and turned around a few of their officials, who have now defected to our side. Our code-breakers decrypted key electronic messages sent and received by both Communist and Jihadist foes."

"From all appearances, our efforts in recent years reaped the richest harvest of intelligence in the history of the CIA and OSS combined. But..." and Booker paused for effect, while somberly gazing at some far off point on the horizon, "things in this game are seldom what they seem."

Booker paused to make sure Rick felt the full force of this last remark. "By early summer of this year I knew something was radically wrong. A team of five agents we sent into the Carpathian Mountains disappeared and have not been heard from in eight months. Many of our operations to establish espionage networks in the Crimea, Georgia and Chechnya were successful in the beginning but eventually collapsed. Our native operatives there were being tortured, assassinated and simply disappearing. Our station chief in Ankara was assassinated by a car bomb. An operation we mounted to land a small army of insurrectionists, demolition experts and spies in Sevastopol—to disrupt, attack and destroy Soviet military units in the Crimea, was intercepted at the landing site and demolished. We received reliable information that many of the covert agents we recruited had been turned and doubled."

Rick was astounded by what he was hearing and couldn't stop himself from interrupting with a question: "Are you saying Mr. Director that Russia and the Jihadists are in league with each other against us?"

"No Richmond, not directly. But you know the old saying, 'the enemy of my enemy is my friend'. The more ruthless the powers pitted against us, the more likely they are to find a way to coordinate certain offensives against their common enemy."

"The FSB, as successor to the KGB, very shrewdly reached out—not to the Islamic extremists fighting to overthrow Assad in Syria—but to one of the secular groups. A spin-off from Al Qaeda, known as the Zorástan Brigade. Zorástan has no religious objective or charter. It is motivated strictly by hatred of Assad, of Israel and, most recently, of the United States. It is a pan-Arabic group which deeply resents U.S. influence in the Arab countries of the Middle East. It's about power, money and oil, not religion. It despises U.S. influence in Saudi Arabia and the other oil-producing emirates on the Persian Gulf. Its preoccupation with power, money and oil gives it a natural affinity with Russia. It has no interest in an Islamic Caliphate, but supports ISIS because ISIS is now an implacable foe of the U.S. and the West. Although it is supposed to be a big secret, our espionage networks have informed us that Soviet Russia and Zorástan have entered into a clandestine, defense alliance."

For a hardcore intelligence analyst like Rick Tallifierro, these revelations, shocking as they were, were a treasure trove. Curiosity got the better of him. "Mr. Director, I can understand why a Euro-Middle East analyst like myself would have a need to know what you are telling me, as background; but hearing it directly from you, rather than at a section briefing, is unorthodox to say the least. Where do I fit into all of this?"

"Well for starters, consider yourself an heir to a revered tradition in Anglo-American espionage circles. I am talking about case officers and agents with the same pedigree and social status reaching out to one another; recruiting each other as operatives and banding together into old-boy clubs composed entirely of spies, counterspies, their handlers and their superiors."

"The two most famous of these bands of brothers are the British-Cambridge alumni group, and the American-Yale University brotherhood. Why this clannish exclusivity? Very simple. Intelligence and counterintelligence require unconditional trust among colleagues. And the only people the aristocratic Cambridge alumni really trust are each other."

"As for the Yale contingent of the Western intelligence fraternity, the only people they completely trust are their follow Yalies. But in the CIA and its progenitor, the OSS, this group was narrowed into a further sub-group: Yale alumni who are also members of the opaque and mysterious 'Skull and Bones Society.'"

As Rick responded, he wore a quizzical expression. He was clearly puzzled by where Booker was headed. "Chief, you lost me. I don't come anywhere near those guys. My parents were far from top drawer and I'm a Georgetown man all the way. I've never even stepped foot on an Ivy League campus."

"You're far more of a thoroughbred than you know. Your father and unofficial uncle, Fred Reitenhauser, were part of the intelligence elite of the Cold War—a legendary core of brave and highly talented military intelligence soldiers. Modesty forbids me from overstating my own role in the MI group. Much of what was accomplished could only have been achieved by sleight of hand. All one need do is look at where our case officers and supervisors wound up after their tours in Munich ended. Besides Reitenhauser becoming a general and eventual CIA chief, his exec in Munich, Art LeBron, wound up his career as head of Homeland Security. Ben Berger eventually became Agent-in-Charge of the Manhattan office of the FBI. After I was poisoned by a traitor in our ranks, your dad became lead intelligence analyst for our unit in 1968. Of course he chose the academic route after the Army but still was a trusted advisor to at least six Directors of Central Intelligence over the years. Warrant Officer Warren Olney eventually became Lieutenant General Olney and was picked by NATO Chief, Gen. Colin Powell as NATO G-2, Chief of Intelligence; at the same time our man, Sgt. Ted O'Malley, eventually a full bird Colonel, served as Commanding Officer of the 409th Intelligence Group. And of course, we all know about Major General Fred Reitenhauser, one of the most universally respected Directors the Company has ever had. This is your lineage Richmond. But instead of being a descendant of an elite social caste, your roots are found in a group of talented and intrepid patriots of the Cold War."

"Well, thank you Mr. Director. That's kind of you. But I only wish that I had the guts and ingenuity of those men. You flatter me by comparing my career to theirs. I'm thirty-seven years old and have spent my career so far in offices, conference rooms and archives in Langley and New York. I've accomplished none of the things those guys did."

"Well you're wrong Richmond. We've had our eye on you since the day you graduated from the Agent Training Center. Your curriculum vitae as an analyst for the last dozen years has been most impressive. I can speak with authority because I was an analyst myself and no job is more important to the defense of the country.

Not much gets past those of us who spend the greater part of our lives here on the fifth floor. We know what's real, and what's bullshit. What's bullshit for one thing is that the politicians and the top brass in the Company, FBI and Homeland Security deserve most of the credit for preventing another 9/11.

"We happen to know that it was you and your staff who warned us in advance of the terror plot on the West Coast and the planned bridge and tunnel bombings in Manhattan. You deserve as much credit as anyone for thwarting those attacks. And your overall tracking of Al Qaeda's plans and operations has been first-rate. With that information we have been able to weaken their infrastructure."

"So, can the modesty and get ready for a major step-up of your role in the Company. For starters we're transferring you from New York to Langley effective Monday morning. I know you like being in Manhattan near that pretty Clarissa, but forget it. We need you here. You've got the weekend to say your goodbyes. To maybe take a bit of the sting out of it, we're promoting you to Chief of the Counterintelligence Section of the CIA, where you'll enjoy the ranking of a GS-18, with a doubling of your salary."

If Rick's jaw had dropped any further, it would have collided with his Adam's apple. So stunned was he by Booker's news and the build-up preceding it that he found himself with his mouth agape and unable to form words, not even "thank you." So he sat for at least a half-minute in numb silence. Booker was clearly amused by Rick's discomfiture and made no effort to stifle the broad smile which had exploded across his face: an expression of fondness for a younger acolyte, mixed with sardonic wit. Yet Booker knew that Rick would gather himself quickly, such was the innate composure infused into the Tallifierros' DNA. That it took him half a minute to respond was merely a symptom of shock and surprise.

"What the hell, Mr. Director. Can you really be serious?"

"I thought I was being summoned here today to either get demoted or canned. Instead, you've handed me the opportunity of a lifetime. I'm overwhelmed. Chief of Counterintelligence? The same job James Jesus (pronounced Heysus) Angleton had. Incredible! As far as leaving New York is concerned, it's a non-issue. Clarissa will understand. She would make the same move if a comparable opportunity in law opened up for her."

"Then great, Richmond; but before you get too enthusiastic I want to give you a reality check. You need to know what kind of a briar patch I'm tossing you in. It's funny that you mentioned the late, legendary Angleton. You'll be crossing and re-crossing his tracks a lot in the coming weeks. But let me not get too far ahead of myself. You need to first be briefed on the conundrum in which we find ourselves.

"I'm all ears, Chief."

Booker rose slowly from his chair, walked to the back of his desk with an air of purposefulness about him (melded with a bit of preoccupation), picked up his pipe and filled it with licorice-blend tobacco. He lit it with a desk lighter inscribed "Munich '68," and without ever raising his gaze to glance at Rick, began thumbing through a file box on his desk filled with 3 x 5 index cards. Finding the object of his search, he lifted a solitary card, read it and stuffed it into an inside breast pocket. Finally, he elevated his gaze, fixed Rick with a stare and spoke in a decidedly lower pitch: "Ever hear of Coriolanus? And I don't mean Shakespeare's play."

"Yes, I've heard of it."

"What have you heard?"

"Coriolanus USA is a secret and subversive organization believed to be composed of a group of former rogue CIA case officers. Their agents allegedly form a motley crew of spies, con-artists, embezzlers, forgers, burglars, and assassins. The sister organization of Coriolanus USA is Coriolanus U.K., a group of anti-western spies and insurrectionists, believed to have been spun-off from Britain's MI-5 and MI-6. The two wings share the same long-term goal: the internal subversion and ultimate overthrow of the governments of both nations by overt attacks and covert acts of treason with strong support of Jihadists in Yemen. They are believed to have provided the expertise and funding for a number of attacks popularly thought of as lone-wolf operations: the Times Square car bomber; the Fort Hood Shooting, the Beltway snipers and the attack on the Boston Marathon. On another tier, they have been active in selling U.S. and British government secrets to the FSB, ISIS, Al Qaeda, and Pakistani Intelligence. The Zorástan Brigade has often acted as the go between and cut-out between on-the-ground operations and Coriolanus. That way Coriolanus has been able to keep its hands clean. Coriolanus USA is believed to be headquartered in Flagstaff, Arizona, and its British affiliate in Manchester, England. But they have cleverly used safe houses and dead-drops in their operations, thereby preventing us from pinning down their exact locations. We believe they are headed up by a top drawer intelligence man, because of the superb quality of their tradecraft. Their use of covers for their training is ingenious: everything from corporate retreats to week-long recreational war games engaged in by middle class white collar and blue collar workers."

"Do you know any details of specific operations?" queried Booker.

"No. So far they've covered their tracks well. What I know about them is mainly anecdotal."

"Ever hear anything about our Russian mole, code named Carlton?"

"Well, just the stuff that's now folklore in the Company. Close friend of Reitenhauser; recruited by him in the early 50s; transferred to us when Reitenhauser moved from Army Intelligence to CIA; our most valuable resource in the 60s during the Berlin crisis and the Soviet invasion of Czechoslovakia."

"Right, those are the basics but you can also add the Cuban Missile Crisis, Reagan's Strategic Defense Initiative and discovery of Putin's blueprints for the Ukraine, to his résumé."

"How did he help us with SDI?" he asked, referring to the *Strategic Defense Initiative* which had been branded by the western media as "Star Wars."

Booker grinned, "Only by giving us hard copies of the specifications for Gorbachev's ICBM missiles manufactured in 1986." A mixture of wonder and professional pride had informed Booker's response.

"Don't tell me he's still operational. He's got to be in his late eighties."

"Ninety-one and still ticking. Oh, he's no longer active in government. He retired twenty years ago, but his knowledge is encyclopedic. He and his family now live in a villa on the Black Sea, miles from anywhere. But he still does some special "consulting" work for us. Reitenhauser was the only agent-handler he ever had; but now you'll be taking over. Effective immediately, he's your resource."

"Ay' Ay' Captain. I'll get right on it."

"Fine. If anyone has any questions or objections, tell them to see me personally."

"Copy that."

"Now, let me move on to another subject." Sensing that Booker was about to broach a more serious topic, Rick doubled-down on his attentiveness, anxious to catch every word and nuance.

"The founder of Coriolanus is believed to be a former station-chief of the CIA operation in Munich in the 60s through the early 80s, who went only by the name of "Q." Q died about ten years ago but not before allegedly spawning a violent network of followers, handpicked and trained by Q personally in espionage, assassination, demolition and the classic "double-cross."

Rick needed no further explanation of the "double-cross. From his own vantage point it was the process by which a high-credibility U.S. case officer doubles an enemy agent and gets him to spy for the U.S. while simultaneously pretending to work for the other side. He is fed some good information as bait.

Hostile intelligence, thinking that the good info being fed to them is the result of their having doubled our man is encouraged to provide even better info, to further burnish the reputation of the supposedly turned U.S. agent—now their agent.

Steadily, the U.S. increases the quality of the intelligence they provide to them, so they think. In fact, most of what they feed them is bogus. Hence, the circle of deception is complete. The U.S. gets solid information from them in return for drivel.

In order, however, for the double-cross to work for the side which initiates it, certain indispensable conditions need be present: First, the initiating agent must be of the highest skill and loyalty, so as to be immune from being doubled himself. Second, the info being fed to the other side to prime the pump must have the *appearance* of being valuable without actually being so. Third, the info coming from the other side must be constantly tested to be sure it is not just part of a ruse to gain the upper hand in the process. Rick was well-versed in the technique.

Booker continued his narrative: "The most notorious case in recent history of the bad guys getting the upper hand involved the elegant Kim Philby. Philby secretly joined the Communist Party in 1934 when still a student at Cambridge. There he was part of an elite social group of upper-class Brits deemed by the hierarchy of British government to be above suspicion. Blessed with the proper lineage and provenance, Philby was, without even trying, a member of the aristocracy—the old boys' club of cribbage, cricket and riding to hounds. The upper management of Great Britain's intelligence agencies, MI-5 and MI-6, salivated at the thought of recruiting Philby and several of his classmates of like credentials. Thus, Philby joined MI-6 in the mid-thirties, and was already a seasoned espionage professional by the time WWII started in 1939. MI-6, the spy arm of British Intelligence, as opposed to MI-5, the counterspy section, knew Philby had joined the Communist Party in 1934 but chalked it up to youthful impetuousness. 'After all', they thought,

'Philby would never betray us. He's one of us. Not only do we trust him implicitly but we don't really trust anyone who is not one of us.'"

Booker puffed ruminatively on his pipe before continuing. "Never for an instant during the pre-war and war years did MI-6 suspect the truth, which was that deep in the marrow of his bones, Philby was a committed Communist and would remain so for the rest of his life. Brilliant and highly competent, he was considered one of the very top stars of Western Intelligence. The truth was that Philby was a double agent working for Soviet Intelligence, an enemy spy and traitor, who—for ideological reasons—owed his unswerving allegiance to Communism and to the Soviet Union, the leading Communist nation."

Booker suddenly ended his oration and grew silent. Rick took it as a signal that the meeting was over.

"Oh, I should have mentioned it earlier, Mr. Director, I've had a tail on me since early this morning. Two male Caucasians."

"Yes, Richmond, I know. Right now they're being berated by the Deputy Director for their sloppiness in letting themselves be made by you. I'll introduce you to them next time you come around."

Chapter Two

CLARISSA

As good as Rick was at compartmentalizing, his thoughts never really strayed far from Clarissa. Now in his mid-fuselage seat on the late shuttle flight back to New York, he was trying to relax by watching the latest film version of "Tinker, Tailor, Soldier, Spy," this one starring Gary Oldman and Colin Firth. While Oldman wasn't exactly Alec Guinness, both the film and his performance were creditable. Author John le Carré, a former British Intelligence agent himself, had never been known to even hint at the real people who inspired his characters. Yet the resemblance between the fictional MI-6 operative, Bill Hayden, played by Colin Firth and the real spy, Kim Philby, was too stark to escape notice.

In the moments before takeoff, Rick hit the speed-dial on his cell phone and after just a single ring Clarissa answered.

Despite his many admonitions not to do so, Clarissa answered the phone in the way she usually did when they hadn't spoken in a couple of days or more. "Well hello, Smiley." The nickname Smiley had nothing to do with a sunny disposition but was an allusion to the

British superspy of le Carré's novels, George Smiley. Given the events of the weekend, Rick decided to ignore the unfortunate, though teasing, connection drawn between him and a legendary spy. Though he always had to be careful, he wanted no discordant note struck between them before breaking his momentous news to Clarissa. In responding, Rick as usual, used his nickname for her.

"Good to hear your voice, Claire."

"And I yours Smiley...missed you."

"Missed you too. What are you up to?"

"Oh, not much; just doing what any lonely and neglected lawyer would do. Writing a brief. How was your weekend?"

"Well, pretty amazing actually."

"Amazing good or amazing bad?" Clarissa knew better than to ask for any details.

"I should be home in a couple of hours and I'll tell you about it."

Clarissa knew from the sound of Rick's voice that nothing bad had happened. She was content to wait.

"I'll order in Italian and a bottle of Chianti to go with it. It'll be waiting for you, and so will I."

"Can't wait. Love you."

"Love you too, Smiley."

Despite the weightier than ever burdens he would be carrying beginning Monday morning, Rick's brief phone conversation with Clarissa reminded him that everything in his life was now just as he wanted it to be. A sense of pleasant anticipation wafted over him. After breaking his news to Clarissa over a cocktail, they would have their own private celebration. A good Italian dinner and then, if all went well, the romance part of the evening would follow. This thought reminded him that the day after tomorrow was Clarissa's 34th birthday. He had better remember to discuss with her making plans to celebrate it.

Though their relationship was sound and (they both hoped) permanent, their demanding careers had thus far stood in the way of marriage. Rick was hopeful that would change soon.

They had long ago discounted the differences in their backgrounds as unimportant. Rick was the son of academics and though his childhood was comfortable, they were far from wealthy. Clarissa on the other hand was the offspring of nouveau riche American capitalists who suffered major reverses thirteen years ago but were already too rich for it to make much difference in their lifestyle or future prospects. Her father, Paul Spence, had been a top executive with Enron until fraudulent accounting practices caused its disastrous downfall. It was December of 2001 while Clarissa was a junior at Vanderbilt University that she learned that her father had taken advantage of insider information to sell his vast stock holdings and options in Enron when its stock was still high. From this crass and calculated act, the Spence family was fixed for life while hundreds of lower rung executives and employees, kept in the dark, were financially ruined when Enron's stock plunged to single digits.

Clarissa was an atypical child of rich and social parents. A studious and idealistic person, she had spurned debutante balls and ski holidays in Aspen for Habitat for Humanity trips to Central America to help organize soup kitchens and free clinics for poverty-stricken children and adults.

The Enron debacle led to a three-year estrangement between Clarissa and her parents. While her father and other executives looked at their insider stock bailout as a privilege of entrepreneurship, Clarissa saw it as an unforgiveable betrayal of the working class, the lifeblood of the company. Now, thirteen years later, though Clarissa had no political affiliation, she still was active in Moveon.org and was an employee-advocate with the two-hundred attorney firm which employed her.

Rick, a political independent, admired his girlfriend's idealism without really embracing it. He had one overriding devotion: loyalty to the CIA and to keeping America safe.

Unlike his father, you could not call Rick an intellectual. He was brainy but not really a scholar. He and Clarissa met at the University of Virginia Law School when he was a third year student and she was still 1-L. Both had excellent grades but as law students there was a major difference between them. Clarissa was energized and thrived in the environment. Rick was bored out of his skull. After classes, Clarissa participated in Moot Court competition, wrote for the Law Review and studied six hours a day. Rick's only competitive activity was the daily gin rummy game in the student lounge. He spurned the Law Review; and two hours a day of study was his max, even the night before exams. After graduation Clarissa passed the Bar exam on her first try, was recruited by, and joined, the Honors Program of the U.S. Justice Department, and two years after that, was hired by Thurman, Bixby and Reed as a highly-touted first-year associate.

Rick blew off the Bar exam, refused all interviews for positions in law and took an entry-level position with the Richmond, Virginia Police Department as an intern in the Unsolved Crimes Bureau. He never practiced law for a single day and his law school diploma hangs in his parents' den along with children's Little League and Pop Warner award certificates.

When asked why he had rejected the field of law in favor of the Richmond P.D., for which a college diploma was not even required, he usually answered, that he didn't think about it much but it was probably because they were good enough to name the city after him.

Rick's real reasons for his dramatic life choice were complex. If it is to be believed that one's destiny finds him, Rick's found him at the Richmond P.D. It didn't take long for the old hands there to realize that he had an uncanny aptitude for going through a dead file, full of witness interviews; blood, hair and fluid specimens; fiber samples, gruesome photos and sometimes blood-stained weapons, and coming up with a working theory of the case. Although the detectives and their supervisors took the credit for Rick's awesome success in solving old crimes, he was the one who got promoted to senior detective with the Unsolved Crimes Bureau and within two and a half years after that to Chief of the Unit. Rick's four years with the Richmond P.D. were among the happiest of his life, but

when the CIA talent scouts came calling, Rick found himself
incapable of resisting their overtures. At the age of twenty-eight he
went off to the CIA training school at Langley, Virginia, without
giving it a second thought.

No small part of Rick's motivation was the off-the-record
assurance given him by the head of the Company's Personnel
Department that there was an opening in the Manhattan field office
and it was his if he wanted it. He wanted it, and grabbed it eagerly.
By then Clarissa was an associate with Thurman, Bixby and Reed.
She and Rick could not believe their good fortune. They were
thrilled to be in New York, together, in love, and enthralled with
their careers. Like most brands of euphoria, however, theirs had a
limited shelf-life.

The first couple of years together in New York were as close to
an unmarried's version of a honeymoon as there was; lots of friends
from their respective jobs, Broadway theater parties, weekend club
hopping, Sundays at the Museums and Central Park, dinner parties,
summer weekends in the Hamptons and Montauk, fall weekends at
West Point football games and skiing in Vermont in the winter.

It was only after they took a five-year lease on an upper-east side
apartment together that a disquiet settled into their relationship.
Although each of them began working longer and longer hours, the
result of increasing job responsibilities, that was not the root cause
of their difficulties; nor was the fact that Rick had no respect or
affection for Clarissa's parents, considering them to be vacuous
social climbers. Clarissa understood because she shared Rick's
opinion in that regard. But they were her parents and she loved
them.

The fact that as they became immersed in their careers, each of
them had less time for the other was not the cause of the growing
unrest either. Each empathized with the other over that fact of their
existences and worked hard at making the time they did have
together as good as it could be.

In fact, the growing strain in their relationship could not be attributed to any external event or circumstance. Rather, it was rooted in who they were as people. Deep in Clarissa's DNA was a powerful current of latent iconoclasm. Like a Rousseau or Robespierre, she instinctively but silently railed against the structures of the society she inhabited. To her they were odious and corrupt. On the outside, she was a role model for an accomplished professional woman, perfectly in tune with her surroundings and worthy of the fruits of her strenuous efforts.

Inside she was an anarchist, one who had experienced the self-realization that she despised the very things about herself that conventional society held at such a high premium. The warring sides of her nature were gradually manifesting themselves in an internal withdrawal proportionate to the degree of effort she exerted to keep her public mask in place. But she could not hide her divided nature from Rick. He knew and loved her too well. Her bipolar behavior was creating an inner recluse, masquerading outside their apartment as a self-possessed extrovert. In their apartment, Clarissa would arrive home with the disposition displayed to her friends and acquaintances during the work day in place. That disposition would usually remain intact during dinner but would gradually begin to dissolve afterwards. Well before retiring for the night she would lapse into a passive, but total, silence.

Rick and Clarissa had been law students at the time of 9/11, ensnared in one of those disciplines like med school, FBI training or the service academies, which turn in on themselves to become micro-societies: self-sufficient, cloistered and so demanding that the student/trainees are removed from the world, physically, socially, and psychologically. Writ large, as if they were isolated aboard a space station, or in an ecologically-controlled bubble. The tragedy of 9/11 did not, therefore, truly register with them.

Clarissa's bifurcated nature was on display long before the Enron debacle. Although presently an extremely attractive woman, as a preteen she was a shy and awkward bookworm who wore thick-lensed glasses to correct 20-400 nearsightedness.

Growing up in Grace Cove, New York, an affluent and secluded community hugging the North Shore of Long Island, with only one road in and out, Clarissa's parents placed her in a series of elite private schools beginning with pre-K. Ninety-nine percent of her classmates all through elementary, middle and high school were Caucasian and one hundred percent were affluent. The environment in one private school after another was status-competitive, socially-inbred and unforgiving as to even the slightest degree of nonconformity. Every student's clothes and accessories bore designer brands. The teenagers drove luxury cars.

From earliest childhood, each student was immersed in a culture for which there was no counterculture. Playing with other children was by prearranged date only, at a tightly supervised playground within the community, inhabited by insiders only. Outsiders were not allowed in and insiders were not allowed out of the community for so long as they fell under the repressive power of parental control. Weekends were spent during the day in children's preteen or teen activities at the parent's private clubs—yacht, golf or mixed activities—and in the evening at social gatherings at either the club or each other's homes.

Clarissa hated the caste into which she was born and began, as soon as she reached the age of reason, scheming to find ways to escape the soul-numbing experiences of affluent suburban life. Public schools were a non-starter with her parents so she began gravitating towards intellectually stimulating and socially useful activities, scarce though they were, in the community. The Public Library was her first refuge and Clarissa at about the age of nine began spending almost every spare hour there. It was a short three blocks from her cliff-top, colonial-style home, overlooking Long Island Sound. Her parents had no real objection. There were two other Spence children, a younger brother and an older sister, and having Clarissa at a safe and supervised location was one less child to worry about, while they pursued boating, golf, water skiing, and day trips with their friends to Manhattan.

Paul Spence would simply slip the librarian a hundred-dollar bill to keep an eye on Clarissa. Her mother, Regina Spence, would arrange for a nanny to stop by the library a few times a day to make sure Clarissa had eaten and hadn't run away from home.

The preadolescent Clarissa read only from the library's approved reading list for children. But she eschewed the Nancy Drew genre in favor of Jane Austen, Louisa May Alcott, Daphne du Maurier, Charles Dickens and the Bronte sisters.

As she entered her teen years she graduated to Joyce Carol Oats, Henry James, Nathaniel Hawthorne, Thomas Hardy and the works of other accomplished women authors such as Flannery O'Connor, Virginia Woolf and Harper Lee.

In her mid-teens, her reading took a sharp turn towards the critical social commentary of the muckrakers: Theodore Dreiser, Upton Sinclair and Frank Norris, letting her imagination write Paul and Regina Spence into the plots as hollow materialists.

Despite her best efforts to maintain a solitary existence, Clarissa blossomed during her junior year in high school at Friends Academy in Locust Valley, about three miles from her home. Providence had granted her the twin blessings of brains and good looks. Her popularity grew almost in spite of herself, as she built a reputation as an innovator-founder of both a debate/forensics club and a drama society. Playing the lead roles in school productions of "The Glass Menagerie" and "Cat on a Hot Tin Roof" made her famous on campus. This was only the beginning. Clarissa's talents and ambition carried her to even greater success in college and law school, her accomplishments bequeathing to her an odd type of prominence, uncharacteristic of most forms of campus celebrity. For though Clarissa earned campus wide fame, by choice she had no friends. Even her roommates were at best casual acquaintances of convenience. Plastered on her face at most times, when in public was a Jacqueline Bouvier Kennedy-type smile, molded from an amalgam of good will, detachment and depersonalization. Somehow, though alluringly pretty, her smile was just forbidding enough to send the sometimes subliminal and other times obvious, admonition: "Keep your distance." In college she disappeared every Friday afternoon after classes and like clockwork reappeared in her dorm every Sunday evening. No one knew or cared where she went or had a close enough relationship with her to ask.

Clarissa's social life, if such existed at all, was a complete mystery. Finally, however, while in law school, the stress and loneliness of the life of a 1-L overcame the walls of her fortress and she allowed a couple of members of her study group, one female and one male, to get close enough to fall into the friend category; or to be deluded into thinking of her as a friend because of their own stress and loneliness. When Rick became her boyfriend, there seemed to be no one who knew whether he was her first, her tenth or her twentieth, not even her parents, who—had they known—would not have cared much anyway.

On Halloween evening as Clarissa, carrying a bag of groceries, walked from the Gristede's Market on Second Avenue and Forty Ninth Street, towards her apartment building on East 51st Street, her thoughts, which usually wandered through a maze of twisted and endless paths once she left her office, were this evening unusually focused on how she would craft a gourmet meal for herself and Rick a little later on. Gazing westbound across Second Avenue, her focus was broken by the sight of Porter Crowe, Rick's former station chief. Crowe lived in McLean, Virginia. What was he doing around here?

Chapter Three

RICK

Rick finished reading the summary of the U.S. Senate Intelligence Committee Report on harsh interrogation methods, including torture, used on suspected terrorists by the CIA. He pondered the conundrum: How to achieve the protection of national security without laying waste to the values of the nation one sought to secure? This enigma would have to wait till later.

Whether brought on by global warming or some meteorological mystery, it was an unseasonably warm early November day as Rick gazed from the apartment balcony out onto the East River. The morning's weather forecasts were predicting temperatures in the high 60s. Laying aside the Senate Committee Report, he tried to give his undivided attention to the day's immediate challenges.

The sights from Clarissa's nineteenth floor balcony were wondrous. All the usual blemishes on the face of Manhattan seemed eradicated. Gone was the carbon emissions haze hanging over the river, which too often occluded the sun. The powerful riverside odors of the fish markets and the river at low tide also seemed muted and benign on this particular morning. Even the cacophony of horns and sirens was far less clamorous than usual. The river itself had taken on a bluish green hue interspersed with sparkles of sunlight.

Rick decided to take his morning Columbian bold on the balcony, from his favorite mug, a stocking stuffer from Clarissa, with "Secret Agent Man" embossed in black Old English script on the side. Although the New York Times sat open on the small patio table revealing the screaming banner headline, "ISIS declares boundaries of New Islamic state," Rick did not pick it up. Booker had called and told him to expect the public announcement so he wasn't surprised. What did surprise him was that he hadn't received a heads-up from his dad first. Tom Tallifierro, with his top secret status as a contract analyst for only the highest priority CIA projects, usually became privy to momentous intelligence a few minutes after Booker did. Invariably, Tom gave Rick a heads-up by a late-night phone call before even Rick's former bureau chief in the CI Section, Porter Crowe, was brought into the loop. Crowe, of course, would now get the news about the same time as the secretarial pool, given his unceremonious expulsion as C.I. Chief—supplanted by Rick with only two hours' advance warning from Booker.

With his feet up on the balcony railing, Rick nursed a slight unease as to why there had been no word from Tom. Yet with his spirits buoyed by his magnificent view of the East River, the United Nations' building, the Fifty Ninth Street Bridge (renamed the Edward I. Koch Bridge) and the cable cars cruising above it, Rick was too pleasantly distracted to worry much. He and his dad would meet anyway at 10:00 a.m. in two hours, on the still-green lawn surrounding the U.N. edifice at the statue of the Prophet Isaiah.

The ostensible explanation for their visit to the United Nations on this beautiful fall morning was to monitor the officials who would show up in the corridors and cloak rooms outside the General Assembly, where the President of the United States was scheduled to deliver an important address on the need for a united defense posture against the ever-burgeoning Islamic Caliphate, known as

I.S.I.S. or I.S.I.L. But this explanation was only a thin cover.

In point of fact, at age 73, Tom Tallifierro's monitoring days were long over. The real reason Rick would be present at the U.N. was that phone calls between persons of interest intercepted by the N.S.A. pointed to a major intelligence leak within the United States U.N. Delegation. Tom was along strictly as Rick's adviser and sounding board. His father's age did not deter Rick in the slightest from asking his dad to accompany him. Tom was in excellent health and had worked in tandem with Rick on prior matters, but only those of great sensitivity and potential danger. From Rick's standpoint there was no better intelligence mind in America than his father and he felt lucky and privileged to be able to draw on his reservoir of knowledge.

Rick walked east on 50th Street from Clarissa's apartment building, turned right on First Avenue and headed toward U.N. Plaza. The U.N. building, a product of early 50s architecture was a sturdy and imposing rectangular skyscraper, reaching into the heavens as if to invoke the aid of Divine Providence in tackling the often intractable problems of ignorance, war, famine and disease.

The U.N. building and grounds were bordered on the east by the East River and F.D.R. Drive and on the west by First Avenue, between 42nd and 46th Streets. Rick, energized by enthusiasm for his present assignment, arrived at the still-green U.N. grounds at about 9:45. Since he was early, he decided to check in with the boss, Former Admiral Wainscott Burns III, the successor to Doug Booker as Chief of the CIA. Though a Naval officer for thirty years, Burns had never commanded a ship. Rather, he went straight from Naval Intelligence training into its Intelligence Division.

At 10:00 a.m. sharp, Rick removed his smart phone from his inside pocket and pressed the speed dial number for Burns. He came on the line only seconds after Rick gave his telephone codename to the receptionist.

"Vanguard, this is Puma."

"Go ahead Puma."

"I'm at the site but Oracle is a no-show."

"Any idea why?"

"No sir."

"Copy. I'll look into it and get back to you. But proceed as agreed."

"Copy that."

Rick gazed distractedly up at the statue of the prophet Isaiah. It wasn't like his father to be late for an appointment. He could not even reassure himself that if something was really wrong he would have heard from his mother. When Tom was out on a mission, no one outside of the Company knew it. Rick's mother probably thought her husband was at the local gym, one of his favorite haunts. Rick's three attempts to reach his father since arriving at U.N. Plaza resulted in his calls being routed into voice mail. He left a message to call him back each time. A twinge of alarm embraced him. Riveted to the base of the statue was a plaque on which words written, for the ages in the Book of Isaiah, were carved and then highlighted in gold paint: "They shall beat their swords into plow shares and their spears into pruning hooks and shall teach war no more."

In the split second it took to read the words "war no more" it happened. A blinding flash of light and fire burst through the foyer and lobby of the U.N. building—a savage rebuttal to Isaiah's sentiment of peace. The prodigious, slower-traveling sound of the explosion followed a fraction of a second later. Shards of glass, shrapnel of concrete and steel, and the flames of Hades, breached the front and side walls of the building; and in their fury, hurtled forward into the morning traffic on First Avenue; and crossed the Avenue, maiming, scorching and killing pedestrians on the west sidewalk. A combination of Rick's location roughly fifty meters from the building and the barrier of the cement prophet in front of him, saved his life. Instinctively, he dropped facedown, when he saw the flash of the explosion and seemed to have sustained only abrasions and minor cuts, together with singed eyebrows.

Screeching brakes, violent collisions, blaring car horns, the thunder of smashing walls and ceilings; screams, moans of agony, shouts of urgency, secondary explosions and loud cries for help formed an orchestra of horror. A dance macabre of pain, terror and death.

As Rick rose on his wobbly legs and fumbled for his mobile phone, a landscape of suffering assaulted his vision: burned, eviscerated and dismembered bodies lay dead, scattered on the ground, all the way to the building entrance; men, women and children on their feet, staggering. Directionless. Propelled only by fear and shock; grass and concrete walks dyed red.

Writhing on the ground, moaning and screaming, were persons of all ages, grievously wounded. U.N. medical personnel were slowly materializing and emerging from who knew where; running and shouting frantically in an effort to help the victims.

The outer walls of the foyer and lobby at ground level and the floor above it were blown away, exposing only a carcass of torn plaster, broken concrete, and twisted cables.

Memories of the front walls of the Alfred P. Murrah Federal Building after the Oklahoma City bombing seared Rick's consciousness with pain and fear of even greater peril to come.

As Rick took a few tentative steps forward, a searing pain assaulted his forehead. The last thing he remembered prior to slipping into unconsciousness was the feel of his fingers exploring the contours of a huge contusion on his central forehead. He drifted slowly through dramatic rainbows of green, blue, orange, sunset red and deepest yellow. He was skydiving without fear, resigned to destiny, indifferent to fate...in free-fall through a dreamed reality, devoid of violence, ugliness and hate.

Chapter Four

TOM

Tom Tallifierro's talents never included direct participation in intelligence operations. He agreed with the commonly held perception that as an intelligence analyst he had no peers, not even Booker, but that he lacked the decisiveness which was an essential quality of a good field operative.

Nevertheless, where exigent circumstances demanded it, he was not averse to slipping into the clothes of a man of action. One of those circumstances had just presented itself.

As the CIA-owned black limousine carrying Tom approached the entrance to the U.N. Headquarters building, it slowed to almost a halt. But before it came to a complete stop, Tom noticed—as he peered through the back curbside window—a familiar figure waiting on the sidewalk. He had to do a double take before the light of recognition went on. The man was dressed in khaki pants and a navy-blue windbreaker, a departure from his usual dark suit and tie. Though both out of uniform and out of context, Tom recognized him after several seconds of doubt. He had met Porter Crowe perhaps a half-dozen times at Langley. Crowe's height (6' 2") and Patrician bearing could not be disguised by mere casual dress. He cut an imposing figure no matter how attired.

Tom's internal data processor quickly inputted Crowe's style of dress, new position as a CIA spokesman and presence at the U.N. building on this particular morning. The synthesis of data yielded only a question: For what possible reason could the Langley-based Crowe—no longer in counterintelligence—but still a resident of Virginia, be alone at the U.N. in civilian skivvies on a workday morning.

Crowe ducked into the back seat of a cab which slowly pulled away from the curb into the First Avenue northbound traffic. Though Tom had spent the greater part of his life as a college professor, moonlighting as an intelligence analyst, his early days in Munich while a Cold War intelligence man had left him with finely honed instincts. He knew intuitively that at that moment it was more important to try to find out where Crowe was headed than to meet his son for their scheduled rendezvous, at the pre-appointed time. Tom ordered the driver to follow the cab and the two vehicles headed north. At 59th Street, the cab made a left and then a short right onto the entrance ramp of the 59th Street Bridge and crossed over the sun-speckled East River into the drab and unfashionable Long Island City section of Queens. The lead vehicle headed out busy Queens Boulevard through Rego Park and Kew Gardens, before finally stopping in front of the Queens County Criminal Courts Building. The limousine stopped about 100 feet behind it.

The cab's engine continued to idle with its doors closed. From the time he entered the taxi cab, Crowe had sat with a cellphone up against his ear, as if engrafted to it. He continued in the same configuration after the cab stopped. It seemed likely he was waiting for someone to appear from one of the court buildings. Tom thought he noticed Crowe stiffen as a lanky man in his middle years, wearing a tweed top coat, sauntered slowly in their direction and approached the cab.

Now it was Tom's turn to stiffen. He spoke to himself in a half-whisper: "What the hell? It can't be! Am I seeing things? He's been dead for 25 years." Tom's brain ran through synapses of logical reasoning: "It can't be him. Even if he were somehow still alive, he would be a quarter of a century older than this guy. But, he could be Jim's doppelganger if it weren't for the age difference. They're about the same height and build too."

Tom quickly set his smart phone on camera function and holding his phone out the window, snapped two profile shots of his target before the stranger disappeared into the back seat of the cab. Looking at the images on his screen, Tom saw that the man had turned his head slightly to the right in the second shot. He looked up quickly to see the two men turn their heads around and stare back at the limo. The dark-tinted glass would have prevented the men from identifying or even getting a description of Tom, but he ordered the limousine driver to drive away quickly, anyway. There was no point in pushing it.

The limo raced south on Queens Boulevard, reached an intersection and made an illegal U-turn into the northbound lane. Without reducing speed, it headed in the direction of the Grand Central Parkway. The cab had also hurdled forward a few seconds after the limo passed it. Tom's binoculars hung around his neck, bolstering his persona as an elderly tourist. He turned in his seat and raised them to his eyes. Custom-made to Tom's specifications, the lenses were powerful enough to allow him to see the new-arrival in the cab lifting what appeared to be a semi-automatic handgun. His muscles froze. But he recovered quickly and ordered the driver to speed it up. Tom kept his eyes riveted on the cab as it approached the same intersection, anticipating with dread a similar U-turn by the cab. But perhaps unwilling to risk either an accident or a traffic ticket for the sake of two strangers, the cabbie sped past the intersection.

Tom exhaled and relaxed but not before ordering the limo driver to drive onto the Grand Central Parkway and back to Manhattan posthaste. The number of ambulances and police vehicles on the parkway passing at top speed, with sirens blaring, was alarming. Tom pushed the speed dial button for his son. After six unanswered rings the call went into voice mail. He tried Burns next with no better luck. On his third attempt to connect with someone, the clipped response of the high-level government pro broke Tom's tension, if only for a few seconds. "Booker." The one word response typified Doug Booker's nonplussed demeanor and confident sense of self.

"Doug, it's Tom. What's going on in Manhattan?"

"Bombing at the U.N. Heavy damage to the first two floors and a lot of casualties. But it appears that the steel girders held and the structure of the building is stable."

"Doug, I was supposed to meet Rick there at the Statue of Isaiah and I can't reach him on my cell. I couldn't get Burns either. You know anything?"

"No, I'm home in McLean. But sit tight. I've got a hotline to the admiral and I'll try to get right back to you." The phone went dead.

The level of Tom's shock and anxiety, if measured like a hurricane or national security crisis, had shot up to a level five as soon as Booker spoke the words, "bombing at the U.N." He heard himself shout, "Step on it," to the limo driver and felt a surge of acceleration; but his senses had otherwise crashed. He no longer heard the sirens of the first responder vehicles or noticed them speeding by and cutting from lane to lane. The limo sped past Flushing Bay, the old World Fair grounds and the new Citifield, home of the New York Mets, without Tom noticing any of it; nor did he notice LaGuardia Airport on his right and the unusual number of police cars and vans crowding its ramps and access roads; police in blue combat gear and National Guardsmen abandoning their blocked vehicles in droves and racing on foot towards the terminals.

Only when the traffic in front of them slowed and stopped on the approach to the Robert R. Kennedy (Previously Triboro) Bridge did Tom emerge from his semi-catatonic state.

Seconds later his cell phone range. It was Booker and he wasted no time. With his best fighter jock's low key delivery, he reported: "Rick was injured in the explosion. A concussion. He lost consciousness and was taken to the NYU Langone Hospital at First Avenue and 35th Street, but they think he's going to be okay." Without betraying the extent of his anxiety, Tom exhaled as waves of relief poured over him.

"Thank you old friend." Doug Booker and Tom Tallifierro had pulled each other out of many scrapes over the last four and a half decades but never had Tom felt more grateful than now.

Wainscott Burns' trip to New York was a far cry from that of your typical shuttle commuter: from private elevator outside his CIA office, to the heliport on the roof, to Dulles International by helicopter, to a CIA jet waiting on the tarmac, to a private landing field at La Guardia Airport and finally by VIP passenger helicopter to the top secret CIA landing pad atop a Central-Manhattan building. He walked into Rick's hospital room fifty-three minutes after hopping on the helicopter at Langley. "Accompanying Burns were two men: a body guard and Mort Fasbender, a deputy from Global Strategies, the CIA think tank division. Already at Rick's side was Tom Tallifierro. Clarissa had not been told of Rick's injury or even that he was at the U.N. when the attack occurred. But intuition told her he was there and she had been frantically calling his cell phone for the past hour, before finally getting through five minutes before Burns arrived. Rick said he was fine and that he was at a "breakfast" meeting at the top of the Marriott Marquis at Times Square when the bomb went off. She didn't believe a word of it but knew it would be futile to pursue the matter. Rick did not disclose his current location.

After perfunctory greetings and introductions, and a few correct inquiries after Rick's condition, Burns launched into his briefing to the Tallifierro father-son duo.

"The bomb is believed to have been made from ammonium nitrate fertilizer, petro-methane and diesel fuel. It was powerful enough to blow out the walls and ceilings of the first two floors without degrading the foundation and structure of the building. The materials used suggest a lone wolf or a small homegrown group rather than Al Qaeda or other major terrorist organizations. So far, eighty-seven are reported dead, including ten middle school students and two teachers on a field trip to the U.N. At least two hundred others are reported injured and fifteen missing. Dead and injured include U.N. visitors; occupants of vehicles and pedestrians on First Avenue; U.N. employees; police officers; foreign delegates and staff members; four clerical employees and two security personnel from the U.S. Delegation. One U.S. delegate was killed, Vivian Frost, as well as a deputy ambassador, Edward R. Childress. One firefighter and a paramedic also died. Fourteen children are numbered among those killed so far."

"The seriously-injured comprise a cross section of the groups in which there were fatalities."

"Of the two hundred or so injured, seventeen are reported in critical condition. The still-missing also include an advance man from the White House and an assistant presidential press secretary, Frank J. Flood. As we learn more, the number of fatalities is expected to rise."

"No one has claimed credit for the attack so far and as of 1:00 p.m., email, phone calls and instant-messaging traffic from the usual terrorist and suspected terrorist groups have been unusually quiet."

"Even though the explosion took place only three hours ago, the fallout is expected to be enormous. So far the shock has held public comments to only a few, but a deluge is expected to begin tomorrow."

Rick's own shock included the matter-of-fact way in which Burns was reporting on a human tragedy and international disaster, as if delivering a prepared briefing to a Congressional subcommittee. The man seemed to have ice water in his veins.

With his father's help, Rick propped his head up on three pillows before speaking. "Anything from the White House?"

"Not yet but the President will be making a statement to be

carried by all major TV networks, plus a half-dozen cable news channels, at 3:00 p.m."

"Dad, if you don't mind, switch on the television to CNN." A second later, Anderson Cooper's face occupied half the screen with CNN's U.N. correspondent, Harris Fitch, on the other half of the split screen. Fitch was apparently in the process of responding to a question put to him by Cooper:

"So far the White House has been mum Anderson, not a word. No leaks to the White House Press Corps; no scoops by any of the news hawks; nothing from the Mayor or Governor either. The only government reaction has come from the Secretary of Defense through a Defense Department spokesman who announced that the national defense emergency alert level has been raised to Defcon 2. This is in addition to public affairs broadcasts on most stations and networks every fifteen minutes warning everyone to stay in their homes until clearance from Homeland Security.

"Would you care to venture a guess, Harris, as to whether this is a sign that another attack is anticipated?"

"I think that's too big a leap to make, Anderson, based on what we know, or more accurately, don't know at this time."

"That was Harris Fitch, CNN's United Nations Correspondent, reporting from the U.N. Headquarters in Manhattan on this breaking story of today's international disaster." Without asking Rick whether he felt up to it, Burns conducted a type of seminar for the next hour, posing question upon question for discussion; mining the gray matter and thought channels of the very fertile intellects of Rick, Tom and Mort Fasbender. Rick was impressed. He didn't know Burns well but today he was witnessing the performance of an impresario of the Socratic Method. Burns laid out for consideration hypothesis upon hypothesis, and then just as quickly skewered each straw man argument he himself had posed. Whether out of deference to his counterintelligence chief or recognition of Rick's superior knowledge and deductive prowess, Burns asked the vast majority of his questions to Rick. Rick's head throbbed as if it were a blacksmith's anvil at the end of the work day, but he stoically suffered in silence. Burns' last question of the day was again directed at Rick: "It would appear, would it not, that since we have not a single lead or clue almost five hours after the bombing, as to the identity of the perpetrators, that N.S.A.'s massive program of surveillance of phone calls, emails and instant messaging has been a total failure?"

Rick sat up straight with his head held erect before answering? "That's not necessarily so Mr. Director. It's been a long time since 9/11 and this is the first major terrorist attack on U.S. soil since then. The Foreign Intelligence Surveillance Act, F.I.S.A., has been largely instrumental in preventing at least eight other attacks, of which I have personal knowledge. I believe it's too soon to draw any hard conclusions from this one. The fact that our enemies have gone mute about this attack leads to several possible explanations."

"For reasons we don't yet know, the silence may be an inherent part of the attack plan itself. Or, our surveillance intercepts may have been expected to hit so close to their core operations, that a total blackout was considered necessary to prevent their exposure. Finally, the communications lock-down could be merely a diversion to distract us from picking up the real trail left by the terrorists." As Burns nodded decisively after Rick's answer, Rick realized that Burns' provocative query was merely a construct—part of the Socratic dialogue of thesis and antithesis.

It would be clear, however, by the next morning that the usual terrorism suspects: Coriolanus, Al Qaeda and ISIS, had gone to ground.

Chapter Five

BURNS

The President's address to the nation from the Oval Office combined solemnity with resolve. The nation, and the nations united, were in deep shock over the brazenness of the attack. The President's brief statement contained no flowery rhetoric or hollow promises to bring the terrorists to justice.

He gave a succinct account of what had happened, the loss of life, the injuries and the damage. He did not speculate about who might be responsible for the heinous act. He summarized the conversations he had with foreign leaders about the attack but confined his own comments to an expression of America's deep sorrow over yet another act of senseless carnage directed at innocent men, women and children. He gave full voice to his own grief but admitted that it was only a "grain of sand in the desert" compared to the grief of those who had this tragic day suffered the loss of loved ones. He ended by pledging "to fight with every resource this country possesses and every ounce of energy he could summon, against those who would cravenly do violence to the just and good citizens of the world." To the guilty parties, he admonished them to take no satisfaction in the evil deeds they had performed because we would fight them unceasingly and would never give up. The entire speech lasted thirteen minutes. The President took no questions.

In the days that followed the U.S. and European media focused almost entirely on the U.N. attack. The mayor of New York City became an overnight international celebrity. Resolutions were passed in Congress and most state legislatures memorializing the victims and declaring solidarity with the peoples of all the countries who had sustained casualties. For the better part of two weeks the political adversaries in America stood united in support of the President and his renewed plan to combat world Jihadism.

But as the wakes, funerals and commemorative ceremonies went forward, the people of America became enmeshed in an emotional outpouring from all quarters of society, some of which threatened to overwhelm rational thought and give vent to a backlash of fury against not only the terrorists but also the nations, ethnic groups and religions with which they were believed identified.

The death toll rose to 99 within the next two weeks. The President and Vice President attended wakes, funerals, memorial services and rallies for peace and justice in places such as Yankee Stadium, the L.A. Coliseum, Manchester Fútball Arena and Vatican Square. Prayer services conducted by Hindus, Muslims, Catholics, Jews, Sikhs and several Protestant denominations were covered daily on T.V. news.

Bills were introduced in the French, Belgian, German, Dutch and Italian legislative bodies to enact laws similar to America's "Patriot Act." New laws were pending in multiple countries by the end of the third week, aimed at enacting rules and regulations against cyber warfare, to expand definitions of terrorism, to broaden the definition of criminal hate speech and to allow greater surveillance techniques through the use of drones, phone taps and email intercepts. Yet after three weeks and despite many highly publicized rumors, neither the FBI, the New York Police nor the

U.N. Investigation Unit had even a single viable clue as to who was responsible for the attack.

In the same three-week period, more than a thousand recorded speeches and statements were made in the fifty states and U.S. territories decrying the attack, empathizing with the victims and criticizing the authorities for their failure to make progress in solving the crime. It was at the beginning of the fourth week that CIA Director Wainscott Burns announced the creation of a joint CIA/FBI Task Force to investigate the incident. He scheduled a top secret retreat for the following weekend at an unknown location, for purposes of launching the task force's mission. He appointed Porter Crowe as Chief Investigator.

During the tenure of Wainscott Burns's predecessor, Douglas Booker, in the wake of 9/11, the CIA had been largely transformed from a traditional intelligence agency to a combination intelligence agency and paramilitary force. Burns was envious of the fact that Booker had received most of the credit for the transformation while he, who had brilliantly headed up the drone program, had labored in obscurity. Now, Burns told himself, it was his turn to get some real recognition and shed the cloak of anonymity for good. Burns' thoughts fused unfulfilled entitlement with wounded pride. His share of public acclaim was long-overdue, though the attack on the U.N. had afforded him the opportunity to finally make a name for himself. In a period of three short weeks he had become the most highly-visible government official in America. But he was shooting for much more than that. He lusted after the kind of fame that had been captured by Eisenhower, MacArthur, Kissinger and Reagan. Burns' ambition knew no bounds. At the age of 59, he had spent his whole life listening to the glowing accounts of brilliance, valor and daring'do of a whole line of Burns Naval officers going back to the Battle between the Monitor and Merrimac. His father, Wainscott Burns, Jr., had served as Executive Officer on the flagship which carried MacArthur's army to a victorious landing at Inchon in 1950. His grandfather, Wainscott Burns, Sr., was a highly-decorated combat veteran of the Battles of Midway and Leyte Gulf. His great grandfather, Sinclair Burns, was part of the U.S. Naval force which broke the Kaiser's hold on Antwerp, thereby supplying Black Jack Pershing with the arms, equipment and materiél he needed for the final push against Germany in the fall of 1918. And his great great grandfather, Prescott Burns, spearheaded an all-out naval assault on Cuba after the explosion of the Maine in 1898. So it went, all the way back to the Civil War. In fact, in the line of distinguished Navy men of the Burns family, the only one whose accomplishments were unheralded and obscure was him, Wainscott Burns III, the current Director of the CIA. He burned with ambition to make his rich wife and four Ivy-League-educated children proud of him. He especially wanted to prove something to his smug and supercilious in-laws and to his own brothers, who had both made a killing on Wall Street. Last but certainly not least there was Deidre, the young woman who lived alone in a stylish apartment off Dupont Circle and to whom Burns had repeatedly promised to divorce his wife. He wanted to be a big success for her most of all.

His family trust fund already paid the rent on her apartment, but that was money earned by his ancestors. He yearned to lavish her with luxuries bought with his own money.

As for Deidre, she had her own agenda which she shared with no other person.

Burns chose as the venue for the weekend retreat of the joint task force the spacious and sequestered Greenbrier Inn in Boulder, Colorado. Everything about the conference was classified: the dates, times, location and attendees, even the fact that there was such an event at all. Burns clamped such a tight lid of secrecy over the proceedings that not only was the national news media clueless about its occurrence, both houses of Congress were kept in the dark as well. The Governor of Colorado was told that it was a special conference of the National Sheriff's Association; and no non-credentialed guests were allowed anywhere on or near the premises.

Rick Tallifierro and Mort Fasbender flew into Boulder together on Friday afternoon, direct from DC. An FBI and a CIA agent were waiting for them at the baggage claim section and quickly escorted them and their luggage to a black Jeep Cherokee with tinted windows. The drive up to the Greenbrier brought back memories to Rick of the one time he was invited to Camp David to brief the President and Secretary of State on what he had learned about Al Qaeda's attack on the London Transit System. Now he was no longer a mere analyst but had risen to the level of one of the CIA's most important bureau chiefs.

Rick found this event to be an even more heady experience than his trip to Camp David. Yet he carried a heavy burden of responsibility because of the most recent assault upon the American homeland; and even more significantly, was troubled by disquieting elements in the manner in which his boss, Wainscott Burns, III and FBI Director, Malcolm Flaherty, were conducting the investigation of the bombing. In the month since the attack it had become clear to Rick that Flaherty's role was greatly subordinated to that of Burns. Flaherty had joined the FBI right after college and had risen through the ranks over a period of twenty-five years, from field agent to Director. He had been an excellent law enforcement officer and an exemplary public servant; but his lack of experience in Washington insider politics had placed him at a marked disadvantage to the savvy Burns, a shrewd and manipulative—some said ruthless— operator. Burns was a master at bureaucratic infighting and even in the short life of the task force had maneuvered Flaherty into a low-visibility position while raising himself to the stature of the face of America's coordinated response to the most recent act of terrorism.

Equally troubling was Burns' affair with Deidre Wilson. Did he really think that with Rick's highly cultivated network of assets and resources, Burns could hide the affair from him? If he did, then that would be either the height of naiveté, or of arrogance. Rick suspected it was the latter. He couldn't care less about the personal lives of others unless they constituted a real or potential threat to national security. The relationship between Burns and Deidre

Wilson clearly did.

Rick's periodic Google searches of "Deidre Wilson" turned up innumerable persons with that name but none of them was the woman involved in an affair with the Director of the CIA. Of course, Rick also vetted her by tapping his vast store of contacts, but all to no avail. No one had ever heard of her and neither the FBI, CIA, NSA, state police departments nor Interpol had even as much as an index card referring to her. It was as if prior to her affair with Burns she didn't exist.

These were among Rick's most troubling thoughts as early Saturday morning he and Fasbender made their way up the winding shrub-bordered path to the regal front entrance of the Greenbrier's main building. Other than a young woman dressed in smart designer jeans and an Adidas ski jacket, walking towards them, the path was unoccupied. The woman also wore stylish sunglasses which effectively obscured her face. But as she began to pass, she suddenly lowered her gaze and stared at the ground. Most people would not have even noticed the quick feint, but Rick Tallifierro, with the well-honed instincts of an experienced counterintelligence man, caught the subtle movement. He turned his head and took in the full face and figure of the passerby. Over the past couple of months Rick had looked at multiple photos of the woman, and even though she wore sunglasses, that did not prevent him from recognizing her. That recognition heightened in him the stunning realization that to one of the most secrecy-shrouded and highly classified gatherings in recent American history, the conference organizer had brought along his unvetted and uncleared mistress.

Chapter Six

CROWE

Rick made one of those split second decisions, born of impulse more than reason. He signaled Fasbender to go on ahead while he turned and began to follow Deidre Wilson down the hilly path. He was gaining on her and would have caught up to her at the point where the path and a circular drive converged, had a government gray, four door sedan, not stopped in the drive in front of Deidre. Even from twenty-five feet away Rick's downward angle provided a clear view of the driver. If Rick was surprised to have seen Deidre, he was stunned by the sight of Porter Crowe, the former chief of CIA Counterintelligence, behind the wheel. And even more astounding was Deidre's opening the back door of the vehicle and seating herself behind the front passenger seat. There were no other occupants.

Would anyone believe him if he related that the beautiful and sexy escort of the married CIA Director was being chauffeured around by the former CIA counterintelligence chief in a government car?

Crowe seemed to notice Rick out of the corner of his right eye but gave no overt sign of recognition. Instead, Rick's presence on the scene appeared to unsettle Crowe, who depressed the accelerator and pulled away leaving a burst of flying pebbles, and burning rubber, in his wake.

A few seconds later Mort Fasbender, who had followed Rick down the path in case there was trouble, reached the driveway.

"What spooked you Rick?"

"It was really nothing. I'll explain later. Right now we have to move fast if we're going to hear Doug Booker's opening remarks to the Conference."

Five minutes later Rick and Mort were flashing their badges to the credentials officer at the front entrance to the majestic ballroom of the Greenbrier. The ballroom was arranged with chairs sufficient to seat five hundred people. The bow-shaped contours of the room allowed every chair to face the dais, where most of the dignitaries of the conference were already seated. As Rick picked up his name tag he saw that neatly printed below his name was the word, "DAIS." He couldn't remember another time during his nine years with the Company that he had been placed at the dais. The other individuals seated there were CIA Director Burns, FBI Director Flaherty, Attorney General Jayne Fremont-Hughes, Director of Homeland Security, Vincent Cuneo, Secretary of Defense, Charles Olney and retired Director of the CIA, Douglas Booker.

Given the hush-hush conditions of the retreat, Rick was pleasantly surprised by the presence of Doug Booker at the conference. Turning to Booker seated to his right, Rick spoke in sotto vóce, "I'm surprised that the Director didn't put Deidre Wilson at the dais too." Hearing this, Booker unsuccessfully tried to stifle a laugh.

As expected, Booker's introduction of his successor was understated, gracious and complimentary. Burns's response was self-congratulatory and classless. He shook hands with Booker only to pose for the cameras at the request of the media. But the cavernous room was full of excitement and bón homme as the more than four hundred intelligence professionals from five federal agencies noisily headed out to their individual caucuses—organized according to occupational specialty, secrecy clearance and need to know.

Burns, Flaherty, Crowe, Tallifierro, Booker and Fasbender did not proceed to any individual caucuses but instead walked into "the Greenbrier Nook," where a table for six was set for a get-acquainted breakfast. A guard was posted at the door of the room to keep everyone out other than the Burns party, the waiters, waitresses and busboys. The six attendees did not discuss business but occupied themselves with small talk as they wolfed down a sumptuous breakfast of fruit, scrambled eggs, toast, bacon, sausage, hot cakes and grits. Rick noticed that everyone ate heartily except Crowe, who mainly pushed his food around his plate while he nibbled on a slice of toast. His apparent new role as a gopher may have taken away his appetite.

Once the morning repast was over, the six men began to wander away but not before Burns made it clear that all of them were expected at his suite for a working lunch at 1:00 p.m. sharp. Rick wondered whether Crowe would have any better appetite for lunch.

Rick and Mort Fasbender meandered in the direction of the Western Frontier Museum, passing a book and periodicals shop along the light-suffused corridor, as the cool strains of Count Basie added to an ambience of elegant pleasure and relaxation.

The banner headline of the Denver Post-Gazette on display in the book shop provided a rude counterpoint to the easy charm of the Greenbrier: "ISIS executes 47 Assyrian Christians in Syria." And below that in smaller bold print, appeared a sub-headline: "Four Middle Eastern heads of state declare their nations at war with ISIS." They were Iran, Iraq, Lebanon and Syria.

Fasbender reacted first: "Not a single day goes by anymore without at least one act of inhumanity against a religious, ethnic or tribal group."

"Yeah," said Rick, "and it all has the feel of being far from random. The attack on U.N. Headquarters was part of it. The daily provocations are deliberate and calculated to cause the targeted nations and groups to retaliate. We're being provoked into war."

Before leaving the Ball Room, Doug Booker had suggested that Rick stop by his room for a chat whenever it was convenient that day. Crowe's odd behavior at breakfast convinced Rick it should be sooner rather than later. The screaming headline in the Post-Gazette told him that meant now. Rick both liked and respected Fasbender and would need him for the mission but intuition told him he better meet with Booker alone.

Rick took the elevator to the fourth floor. Before exiting he sneaked a look in each direction. Other than a noisy family composed of early-graders and harried parents, nothing unusual appeared to his left. To the right about forty feet down the hall stood two chambermaids arguing in Spanish with a guest who was venting a grievance about no clean towels in his room. Rick hoped that nothing more eventful than these small human comedies would confront him as he walked towards Doug's room at the end of the corridor. He had more than a few misgivings about meeting privately with his mentor on the occasion of Burns' big coming out party. But he made it to Booker's room without running into anyone he knew.

Doug Booker, looking ten years younger than his age, greeted Rick at the door to his room. He wore blue jeans, moccasins with no socks and a New England Patriots t-shirt.

"Glad you could make it, Rick. I don't intend to stick around this dog and pony show much longer and I thought it important for you and I to have a one to one chat."

"You mean you're going to miss Burns' mandatory lunch?" said Rick, with a bit of bemused irony in his voice.

"Well I'm sure Burns wants me there but if he thinks he can compel it, he's been reading too much of the Agency's propaganda, he himself wrote. By 1:00 p.m. I expect to be boarding a Southeast

Airlines flight, nonstop to Boston. I don't want to confuse anyone into thinking I'm not retired."

"But I gather you'll be coming out of retirement for the next hour or so," Rick ventured.

"Yes, but only because of what we used to refer to on CIA field operations as "exigent circumstances.""

"Okay, now you've really gotten my attention; what's up Mr. Director?"

"Rick, recall the briefing I gave you at Langley in the early spring when I told you about your promotion. That was an introductory course only. Today's briefing is the advanced seminar. Some of what I am going to tell you may be hard to believe but I've known you all your life and you know I won't be just blowing smoke."

"In that I have every confidence."

"First, tell me how the investigation's going." Rick stiffened and made no attempt to suppress the look of frustration which crossed his face. But he felt comfortable revealing his annoyance and frustration to Booker, no less so than if he were confiding in his own father.

"The usual suspects, Coriolanus and its evil progeny have apparently gone so deep underground that it's as if they don't even exist. Not an intercepted phone call or email, no sightings, no press items. Nothing. The legend is that before Coriolanus waded into international subversion and terrorism, it was a troublemaker for hire used by diverse cults and movements. It had no interest in their causes but needed the money to grow their organization. One of their biggest clients was a Mormon group in Utah dedicated to protecting polygamy colonies—by deception and subterfuge—from interference by law enforcement.

To stay out of reach of the Utah authorities, Coriolanus established its base of operations outside of Utah in nearby Flagstaff, Arizona. It seemed like an odd location but it worked for them so they just stayed. For the most part they maintained their anonymity by wide use of cover names, post office boxes and dead-drops. But every now and then the FBI or Treasury would pick up their trail. Surveillance and arrests would follow but they were never able to make anything big stick. Coriolanus's use of cut-outs in their activities and communications were so sophisticated that the Feds usually wound up chasing their tails whenever they went after the suspected higher-ups. But those ineffective pursuits were nothing compared to the way things have been since the U.N. attack. Our electronic and paper trails have dried up. Former safe-houses in Flagstaff are either boarded-up or occupied by someone else. Even their sub-organizations' vehicles have fallen off the grid. No new purchases, leases, registrations, reported accidents or even traffic tickets.

FBI has pulled in all its informants in the area and put the screws to them. They say they know nothing and have stuck to their stories."

"Where do you suppose Coriolanus acquired such skill in clandestine methodology?" Booker interjected.

"That is a question our people have never been able to answer."

"Yes, but what do you think?"

"Well, it appears they've been trained in classic KGB tradecraft but none of the U.S. investigative or counterintelligence people have ever made the connection. So, I don't know."

"How did you become so personally invested in this thing?"

"By default. Investigating acts of terrorism is not my thing. It's more for Homeland Security, the FBI and regional police forces. But the people Burns has put in charge are a joke. Flaherty is his minion and Crowe is a burned-out case. I need to pursue the investigation as an essential part of my counterintelligence mission because if I don't, nobody else will. Since Crowe is nominally in charge of the investigation, I can't be seen as preempting him; so I'm running it off the books with my own people."

Booker showed no signs of shock or surprise at this information. He merely nodded and stated knowingly, "It's probably better that way." Rick was surprised by Booker's reaction. "I don't understand, Doug, how anything about this half-assed situation could be for the better."

"That's because you don't know what you need to know to make the right assessment. For that matter, Burns might not either and I know Flaherty doesn't. The only people who know for sure are the President, his national security adviser and myself. At the President's request, you are to be brought into the loop as well."

"Let me start by saying that the official investigation of the U.N. attack and your unofficial one are misdirected—the reason being that through no fault of your own, you're starting at the wrong place. By 'deductive' reasoning you're starting with the attack itself; and working backward to find the causes and identify the perpetrators. This is a maladaptive approach which is doomed to failure. What you need to do is start at a particular time in Twentieth Century history and work your way forward to the present."

"Sounds interesting, tell me more."

"To begin, the time and resources you have spent chasing Coriolanus have not been wasted."

"That's good to know," said Rick with a hint of sarcasm.

"But not for the reasons you think. It hasn't been wasted because it will now be easier for you to accept one of the central truths of the situation, which is that there is no Coriolanus and never has been."

Rick felt his face and neck take a sudden surge of heat from a spike in his blood pressure. Was Booker just putting him on? No, he wasn't the joking type. But what was he talking about? If it were almost anyone but Booker, he might conclude that the man had lost it completely. Yet, there was Booker looking directly at him with his trademark expression of somberness mixed with sincerity.

"And?," said Rick.

"And what?" replied Booker.

"And what, you ask! Less than thirty seconds ago you told me that a nefarious terrorist organization, the number one target of American law enforcement and the CIA's counterintelligence program, doesn't exist; like Santa Claus and Superman don't exist. Would you care to explain?"

"Of course," said Booker, striking the look and tone of one seeking to mollify a less informed person. "Coriolanus" is an invention. A construct. An elaborate hoax, created by deep-cover moles working for decades for enemy intelligence. Its function is to deceive and divert all of us from learning the identity of our real enemies—not just the U.N. bombers—but the cyber terrorists who have hacked into Defense Department and J.P. Morgan Chase computers; the saboteurs who blew Flight 808 out of the sky over Jamaica Bay in New York more than a decade ago; and the assassins who murdered former CIA Director William E. Colby years before that. Cleverly, they made it look like death by natural causes. Add to that the massive leaks of U.S. government secrets to hostile governments and organizations, going on for more than fifteen years before anyone ever heard of Edward Snowden or WikiLeaks."

Rick, by a sheer act of will, maintained his composure. "If you don't mind my asking, Mr. Director, why didn't you tell me this when we first discussed Coriolanus earlier this year?"

"You weren't ready for it."

Choosing not to waste time exploring the implications of that cryptic answer, Rick let it go.

"If there is no Coriolanus, who has been committing so much mischief and mayhem for the last twenty-five years?"

"We don't know and it will be your mission to find out and to stop it. What we do know is that Coriolanus is a brilliant fabrication. It has its own post office box, phone number with voice mail, corporate charter as a 501(c)(3) charitable organization, email address, website and Twitter page. Scratch below the surface of any of these clever artifices and you will find the names of incorporators, P.O. box renters, directors and officers. The individuals in control of these entities share three things with each other: First they all have social security numbers, drivers' licenses and credit cards; second, they each file annual income tax returns;

and third, they don't exist. They are totally fictitious.

"But what about having their base of operations in Flagstaff and the British chapter in Manchester?"

"Complete ruses; inventions and subterfuges. Cover stories that they have managed to maintain by sleight of hand. For example, they have used actual street addresses from time to time. But visit the locations and all you'll find is a clueless building manager in his seventies who answered an ad on Facebook to get his job, has never met his employer, and is paid each week by an electronic cash deposit directly into his checking account. He communicates with his boss by email only. Never having spoken with or seen him, he is unable to provide any useful information. His job is off the books and he doesn't get a W-2 form."

"But what of the perpetrators we've caught over the years?"

"They were all hired, given instructions and paid by the same method as the building managers; and knew equally as much, which is nothing."

"We've tried to dig deeper to levels below the ones I've just described, only to find another cut-out. Multiple layers of bogus information and organizations have been piled on top of each other for more than three decades."

"But shouldn't we still be digging anyway?"

"No, the President has decided it's nothing more than an expensive exercise in futility. As I said, you will need to abandon the practice of starting with the present crisis and searching laterally or backwards. Instead, you need to start in the past and move forward until you reach the present. Hopefully, you'll solve the mystery along the way."

"Where do you suggest I start in the past?"

"To answer that I'll need to give you a little history lesson.

Fortunately, as a trained and experienced counterintelligence man you already know some of the history, but not all of it. Especially not all of the important stuff."

"So here goes, and you'll have to rely on memory, because you can't take notes."

"You already know something about the man who may have been Great Britain's worst traitor, Harold Adrian Russell Philby, known simply as Kim Philby. Philby was one of a group of elite Cambridge graduates, most of whom had their roots in the British aristocracy. The majority of them were scions of rich men, Lords and Nobles who were considered the leadership class of the nation. Cambridge graduates permeated every facet of government, and the British Secret Service was no exception. They and other members of the aristocracy were the ruling class of British Intelligence. This is not surprising because intelligence work requires absolute trust and the ruling elite trusted each other without reservation. The Cambridge set of the mid-1930s produced many of England's espionage heroes, such as the great Nicholas Elliott—a close friend of both Philby and Angleton—but also produced a group of hardcore traitors.

The mid-30s was the worst period of the great Depression. Academics at universities everywhere blamed the excesses of capitalism for the Depression and many flirted with Communism. For some it was simply a temporary phase; for others such as Philby it was a total commitment. Communism became Philby's religion. Its roots were planted deep within him and he adhered tenaciously to its tenets for the remainder of his life.

In 1934 Philby joined the Communist Party; and thereafter never renounced his membership.

Philby and Elliott both joined MI-6, the clandestine intelligence-gathering branch of British Intelligence, in 1939, right before the outbreak of World War II. The two Cambridge alumni, both members of the British upper class, hit it off at once and became fast friends. Philby was elegant, sophisticated and charismatic. He displayed a remarkable talent for deception and bold action. Together, Elliott and Philby pulled off some of the most brilliant and high-yielding spy operations against Hitler and Nazi Germany of the entire war.

During World War II, the two added another elite member to their small circle of spies—the highly intelligent and audacious American counterintelligence expert, James Jesus Angleton.

Though supremely competent in his own right, Elliott hero-worshipped Philby. He was fascinated by the fact that while Philby possessed great clarity of mind, he had liberated himself from the dry conventionality and stifling rules of the British intelligence services. Philby eschewed the Whitehall Street spats, stiff collar and pin stripe. As a man of action rather than theory, he built his own distinctive persona. Such was especially manifested by his style of dress, which included a tweed jacket with elbow patches, a cravat, suede shoes and a Homburg. Topping off his sartorial swagger was an ebony-handled umbrella. He knew that one needed a distinct, self-created persona in order to be a successful agent and became the paradigm for the new breed of stylish intelligence agents. Following his example, the rigid formality of the old-style case-officers gave way to new classes of recruits, casually attired in expensive gray flannel trousers and sweaters. Instead of gathering in men's clubs, many of the new breed opted for bars and cafés, boasting of their conquests and underworld contacts. While the old set of British intelligence officers had a gentleman's reserve about them, the new Turks led by Philby had panache. Heavy drinking and raucous behavior among the new breed was not uncommon.

Unlike the dashing and stylish young men of MI-6, the agents of MI-5, the counterintelligence branch, were generally more conventional, conservative and sober. With a few exceptions, they dressed plainer, acted with more dignity and drank less. The parallel to MI-5 in the United States is the FBI, whereas the parallel to MI-6 is the CIA.

Philby and Elliott were men of exceptional talent and versatility, leading them to be assigned to the special counterespionage section of MI-6, known as Section V.

There they doubled several enemy agents during World War II and learned from them the identities of top spies working against the allies. Liquidation of these hostile agents followed in due course. Philby, Elliott and their compatriots did serious damage to the Abwehr, Hitler's intelligence service, turning it from a sleek and efficient engine into a piece of broken machinery. At Bletchley Park, British intelligence experts broke the Germans' secret code.

Facing defeat in 1939 at the hands of the Germans, several members of Poland's intelligence service escaped and defected to Great Britain. There they shared with British Intelligence the progress they had made in deciphering Germany's secret code. Using the information provided by the Poles and pooling it with the results of their own espionage, the Brits made a model of the machine the Germans used to encrypt messages to their military units and intelligence agents. The machine they employed was named "Enigma." They were also successful in getting hold of the manual for the German machine and its code settings.

The Brits advanced their use of Enigma by learning to decrypt and read the German Army and Abwehr's coded messages. They called the information which fell into their laps as a result, "Ultra."

"The world was amazed at how long England was able to hold Hitler's forces at bay, given the Nazis' superior numbers in personnel and weaponry. The fact that they were able to hold out until America came into the war can be partly attributed to Enigma and Ultra, which in turn owed much of their effectiveness to the efforts of Philby, Elliott, Angleton and other stars of the British Secret Service and America's intelligence arm, the OSS.

To maximize the effectiveness of Enigma, the Brits planted misleading clues in German communication channels and then employed Enigma and Ultra to gauge the reaction of the German High Command to the planted information. The loop of deception was complete.

The British and Americans were using espionage in exactly the way it was designed: to compromise the security of the enemy's communications while protecting the security of their own. The real brains behind the fictional Coriolanus have operated in the exact same way.

I don't mean to suggest that Philby, Elliott and the rest of the Cambridge set owed their success to Enigma and Ultra alone. They were also highly effective in luring defectors from Germany, who were treasure troves of valuable intelligence; capturing German spies in England and turning them against the "Fatherland"; planting false information with the Abwehr as to where the invasions of Italy and France would take place. And the OSS, new to the spy game, was learning fast. Angleton and his team even helped the Partisans in Italy capture Mussolini.

At MI-6, the top people were almost giddy with success. Elliott and Philby were attaining hero status and their careers were skyrocketing. But in the midst of the euphoria a creeping cancer was at work, largely undetected. Philby was a double-sided man. At the same time that one side of him was running, or participating in, brilliant operations against the Germans, his other side was a Soviet spy. His Russian case officer, who would defect to the U.S. after the war, was the enigmatic Anatoly Golitsyn.

Philby is believed to have passed on to the USSR virtually all important intelligence information which came into his hands from the early 1940s through the early 1950s.

To his bosses at MI-6, it would have been appalling had they known that Philby was passing on such secrets to the Soviets, even though Britain and the Soviet Union were technically allies during World War II. Anyway, it didn't stop after the war. Philby then began passing on to his Soviet handlers information gained by him from the U.S. and other future NATO members. For more than a decade he shared with Stalin the identities of agents and case officers, a detailed chart of the very structure of the British and American secret services and their clandestine operations."

"Philby's loyalty was always first and foremost to Moscow, but because he was one of them, the Cambridge boys at MI-6 apparently never suspected a thing until after the real damage had been done. Philby was Elliott's closest friend and Angleton's mentor. Yet neither of them suspected his treachery until the 1950s. When they were finally forced to recognize that he was a traitor and had betrayed them personally, it was a great psychological shock to each of them, which had life-altering impacts on their individual opinions of human nature and their views of the intelligence game in general."

"But, Rick, if this story were only about Philby, we could end it right here and you may or may not have been entertained by it, but hardly enlightened. Our present predicament has its roots in this story, so bear with me a while longer. Philby was a charming Pied Piper sort of fellow whose charisma attracted many more acolytes than just Elliott and Angleton.

Have you ever heard of the Cambridge Five?"

The early history of the OSS and MI-6 was not exactly emphasized in Rick's CIA training, so his knowledge of the Cambridge Five was merely anecdotal.

"Well," replied Rick, "all I've really heard is that they were double agents from MI-6 who were turned by Soviet Intelligence; and that Philby was one of them."

"That's basically true but not the whole truth. First, only four of the alleged five were ever identified with any degree of certainty. Though the names of many candidates for the number five position were bandied about, that was mostly speculation and guesswork. The other four were Philby; his friend, Guy Burgess of MI-6, a communist and handsome drunk who was also a promiscuous homosexual; Donald Maclean, a clever linguist and British spy with the Foreign Office; and their friend Anthony Blunt, a Cambridge art scholar ensconced at the heart of MI-6. All four eventually defected to the Soviet Union.

But it is the never-identified "fifth man" of the quintet who is the central player in our little drama. Though we do not know the identity of the "Fifth Man," we have been able to piece together bits of intelligence from Russian defectors and convicted Soviet spies, such as the Americans, Aldridge Ames of the CIA and Robert

Hansen of the FBI. When added to what our espionage agents have
learned over the last fifty years, the bits and pieces of intelligence
paint an unfinished portrait of a young American employed by one
of our intelligence organizations, who was close to Philby at the
time of the latter's 1963 defection to the USSR. He would appear to
have known Angleton too because there was no one in U.S.
intelligence in the 50s and 60s Angleton didn't know. We suspect
strongly that the Fifth Man was turned by Philby and handpicked by
him as his successor upon Philby's defection. We also have
intelligence to support the inference that the Fifth Man was a Yale
graduate, probably of the Class of 1960. He became and still is a
deeply embedded mole who has worked diligently against our
interests for the last half century."

"But if we have known of his existence for so long, how has he
been able to work so flawlessly without eventually being caught?"
Rick asked.

"We've only known about him since Ames and then Hansson
sang, about twenty years ago. But, more importantly, we believe he
was mentored by Philby, who designed his cover. The master
planted the mole under deep cover, but before that tutored him in the
arts of deception and living a double existence. Remember, Philby
fooled the British, the Germans, the Russians and the Americans at
the highest levels for more than 15 years. Ironically, Philby was
thought by Moscow to be lying to them while he told them nothing
but the truth; and MI-6 believed Philby was honest with them, yet he
lied to them consistently for decades.

It, therefore, comes as no surprise to us that the Fifth Man,
Philby's student and protégé, has been able to pull it off.

After an intensive in-house review of our biggest fiascos over
the past twenty years, we concluded that in one way or another the
Fifth Man and his small but lethal team, have partially orchestrated
everything from the disaster at the Munich Olympics, to the
skyjackings and the crash of Pan Am 103 at Lockerbie; to the two
attacks on the World Trade Center; to the armed incursions in the

southeastern Ukraine, and Crimea; plus most acts of terrorism on American or British soil since 9/11. The reason they've been able to pull off so many incidents is their mastery in creating multiple levels of insulation.

I reported to you the last time we met, that major CIA operations for years have been compromised. Philby managed to harpoon most British anti-Soviet operations after World War II and through the Korean War; and the "Fifth Man" picked up where he left off. The latest attack on the U.N. bears all the earmarks of a Fifth Man-created and orchestrated event.

Now that I'm retired, it's going to be up to you and your off-the-books team to take up the mole hunt. Burns and Crowe are so out of their depth that we couldn't hear them if we used sonar. I recommend strongly that your first step should be to fly to the Crimea to meet with Carlton. He knows that you're his new control and he's eager to meet you. You won't regret making the trip; though since the Crimea has been annexed by Russia, you will need to go in under cover. Whatever you do, don't let Burns find out about it. I'm not sure I trust him, especially with his suspicious new girlfriend, although I suspect he may be a mark rather than a player."

"Do you think it's possible, Doug, that the Fifth Man could be a woman?"

"We don't think so but, yes, it's possible. What's also possible is that the original Fifth Man trained a successor, or more than one. After all, he would be about 75 now; and the audacity of his operations over the past 15 years suggests that the most active mole may be a younger man. Oh, and Rick, be careful. He's deadly. When former CIA Director Bill Colby was found dead in the waters near his home in 1996, it was reported as a stroke or heart attack. We always believed it was a homicide. Colby knew Philby well from their World War II days when Colby was in the OSS; and they worked together on double-cross operations. But he was nowhere near as close to Philby as Elliott or Angleton and never exercised the same restraint in voicing his suspicions. When the head of MI-5 was closing in on Philby, there were persistent rumors that Colby was one of their informants. Philby lived in the Soviet Union from 1963 until he died at the age of 76 in 1988. It is not beyond the realm of possibility that he ordered Colby's assassination. The best information we have is that Philby continued spying as a double agent on the NATO nations after his defection in 1963 and up to the time of his final illness in 1988. He was so celebrated in Moscow, where he served as both a NKVD and KGB operative, that in 1990 the USSR issued a commemorative stamp with his portrait on it.

Philby conned the British, the Germans, the Soviets and us. Incredibly, he still held the honor of being a member of the Order of the British Empire in 1969, six years after his defection to the USSR.

The utter failure of British and American intelligence to expose and capture Philby was a catastrophe of Herculean proportions. God knows how many lives were lost as a result. The ripple effect of Philby's diabolical scheming undoubtedly extended the length of the Cold War. For how long is anyone's guess.

You, Rick, now have an opportunity to right some of the wrongs that were done as a consequence of our predecessors' stupidity. You can never undo the damage that was done, but if you can catch Philby's evil progeny, you may be able to protect many other innocent lives from Philby's followers.

But all of this is about more than just Philby. Remember, go back and then move forward. Carlton should be helpful in telling you how far back to go and how deep to dig. Also, never lose sight of the malevolence of Islamic Jihad and its central role since no later than 1993.

Chapter Seven

RICK AND CLARISSA

Rick's flight to DC from Colorado was his first return trip home. Of course he had returned many times to his parents' home and to his own apartment, but never to the home of Mr. and Mrs. Richmond Tallifierro of Bethesda, Maryland. Rick and Clarissa had been quietly wed a week before he left for the Greenbrier, in a civil ceremony at Manhattan Borough Hall. Rick's best man was his brother, Fred. Clarissa's maid of honor was her law school roommate, Cynthia Torres, now an Assistant U.S. Attorney with the Criminal Branch of the United States Attorney's Office, Eastern District of New York.

A small dinner celebration was held afterwards at Tavern on the Green, attended only by the newlyweds, best man, maid of honor and the parents of the bride and groom.

Rick had been splitting his weeks after his release from the hospital: Monday and Tuesday in Langley attending to his administrative duties as C.I. Section Chief and Wednesday through Sunday in Manhattan, supervising his secret investigative team.

The shock and horror of the bombing at the U.N., Rick's injury, the frenetic activity by federal, state and city law enforcement agencies, the resultant new legal problems flooding Clarissa's law offices and Rick's all-consuming duties in the wake of the attack, deeply affected both Rick and Clarissa. The entire country was on a war footing with the front lines located in New York City. And although things were never simple between Rick and Clarissa, it was clear that mystical ties of love, worry and shared purpose had bound them more tightly together—like soldiers joined in a great battle. After years of indecision and drift in their relationship, the tragedy at the U.N. had ironically welded a partnership for life. It was a pity that it took an international tragedy to do it.

Rick and Clarissa had signed a lease for a condo in Maryland on the outskirts of Bethesda, just inside its city limits. But they split their time between two venues, New York and the DC area. Clarissa retained her Manhattan apartment as their New York residence. Clarissa and Rick spent occasional weekends in Bethesda and wished it could be more.

The long flight from Colorado to DC had allowed Rick to assimilate the astounding information given to him by Doug Booker. Rick was well aware of the brilliant service given by Booker to his country for the last sixty years. He knew that not a word of what Booker said was untrue. Yet he was troubled. His uneasiness had to do with something his father-in-law, Paul Spence, had said to him at the celebratory dinner after the wedding.

As Rick returned to the table after a visit to the men's room, Spence intercepted him and insisted they have their own private toast for the occasion in the bar.

Rick did not particularly like Spence and would have passed on the drink had the latter not firmly grabbed him by the elbow and steered him towards the bar. Spence was, in fact, his father-in-law now and in the interests of family harmony, Rick did not resist. Spence ordered two Rob Roy scotches, neat, without asking Rick what he wanted. Such was the nature of the man: domineering, aggressive and thoughtless.

The conversation in the beginning was desultory small talk about Long Island's high school lacrosse teams, the soon-to-be-vacant Long Island Coliseum, since the Islander's Hockey Team moved to Brooklyn and the new Mayor of New York City, Bill DeBlasio, for whom Spence held open contempt.

It was when Rick drained his glass and turned his bar stool in the direction of the exit that Spence suddenly changed the subject. "So Rick, has the great man told Burns that you should be running the U.N. investigation instead of Crowe?"

CIA officers were trained not to show surprise but Rick doubted that his facial expression, upon hearing this utterance by Spence, masked his shock.

"That's classified information Paul and I cannot discuss it."

But as Rick spoke, Spence was already signaling the bar tender for a check.

Spence smoothly slid his Amex platinum card across the bar while he waved and smiled at some acquaintance at the other end. Almost simultaneously he rose to shake the hand of another acquaintance edging his way in their direction.

Rick decided he didn't want to be introduced, so he simply rose and walked back to their table. He didn't care whether Spence liked it or not.

Now, after his meeting with Booker, the premise of Spence's statement that "the great man" wanted him to lead the investigation had been confirmed. But how could Spence have known that, even before Rick himself knew it?

Booker was referred to as the "great man" by a small coterie of seasoned intelligence insiders, which did not include Spence. Or did it? Booker was one of the most tight-lipped men Rick had ever known—famous for commenting on work-related matters only for a specific objective, solely on the matter at hand and only to those having a need to know. His reticence was calculated and had enabled him to survive in a profession fraught with peril, for sixty years.

As his plane began its descent to a landing at Ronald Regan International Airport, Rick's mind ran through his options. He could question Booker about the source of the information. Not a great option. Booker contacted you, not the other way around. Another option was to confront Spence. But he had no confidence Spence would tell him the truth, and at the same time Rick would have betrayed his concern; probably not in his best interests.

On the other hand, Spence's remark seemed calculated rather than an inadvertent slip. Rick's best option, he decided, as the plane touched down, was to do nothing for the time being. If Spence had calculated his remark, he would be waiting for a reaction of some sort. When he didn't get one, by words or action, he was likely to devise a follow-up. Spence never let anything just drop.

The opening of a new session of Congress on January 21st injected a blast of energy and excitement into the previously languid U.S. Capitol. Rick and Clarissa had not had a honeymoon so decided to spend Friday night through Monday just for themselves.

It was clubbing with friends in Georgetown on Friday night, a trip to Annapolis on Saturday, where they enjoyed a lobster dinner at their favorite seafood house, and a night at the luxurious "Midshipman Inn." After their return to Bethesda on Sunday morning they spent a day just lounging, sipping expresso, reading the newspapers and brunching on bakery-ordered croissants, as the spirit moved them. But most importantly they just talked. They may have missed an official honeymoon but were honeymooners nonetheless. The gloom which had always seemed to hover just above Clarissa's head appeared gone. The banishment of all outside distractions, at least for a few days, opened the way for the arrival of an intimacy neither of them had enjoyed in years. As they chatted there seemed no room for the interlopers of danger, loneliness or sadness. The singular sense of duty each of them felt was to the other only. They talked of all sorts of things: their lives growing up, the pain of adolescence, the search for a true relationship—a melding of shared interests, emotions and compatible world views. How blessed they were to have found these things in each other; and how fortunate they were that they had perfected their union in marriage.

Although Rick and Clarissa had lived together for years, never before had they approached the level of intense love and intimacy they were enjoying this weekend.

How long could their blissful state last? As a couple, they were a counterintelligence specialist and a tough civil litigator, both well into their thirties. They held no illusions that it could last forever, but could not have predicted how soon it would be rudely shaken.

Monday saw them take a relaxing drive into the Virginia foot hills of the Blue Ridge Mountains and then back to Mount Vernon on the Virginia side of the Potomac. They had reservations for dinner at the Mount Vernon Inn situated on a bluff overlooking the Potomac, with an awesome view. They arrived early enough to have cocktails at the bar before dinner.

Their champagne cocktail glasses tinkled softly as they toasted each other and pledged their mutual and enduring devotion. After two drinks each, they asked the maitre'd to seat them at a table near the limestone fireplace, but in a secluded corner of the restaurant. Being who they were, they both began to relax their pledge not to discuss work for the entire weekend. It had been a full seventy-two hours since either of them had spoken a single word about their jobs, but now Rick was the first to break their mutual vow.

As the captain assigned to their team of waiters lit the candles on their table and the steward handed them wine lists, Rick's mind wandered to a different, but still innocuous subject.

"I saw Crowe at the Greenbrier conference."

"Oh really, did you speak to him?"

"We exchanged a few pleasantries at breakfast the day after I got there; but that was it."

"How did he look?"

"Harried, distracted and diminished."

"Diminished?" Clarissa asked, somewhat perplexed. "What do you mean by diminished?"

"Oh, I don't know; I guess it's just that his former strong personality seems to have gone into eclipse, as he's metamorphasized from a leader to a lackey."

This prompted a hearty laugh from Clarissa as she sipped her third champagne cocktail and then polished it off in a single swallow. Her bemusement continued as her eyes lit up and she chuckled softly, even as Rick was sipping from a glass of Chablis from a bottle provided by the wine steward.

After placing their dinner orders, Rick nursed his first glass of wine while Clarissa downed hers in only a few gulps. Her eyes still danced with amusement, although something else was now competing with her lightheartedness, as a look of nervousness appeared in the tightening of her facial muscles and quick flickering smile.

"Well," said Clarissa, "as much as I am disinclined to revel in the misfortunes of other, in the case of Crowe, it couldn't have happened to a nicer guy." This time there was no mirth accompanying her remark. "So tell me more about Crowe. Who did he hang out with in Colorado?" Rick was beginning to regret having brought up the subject. "Oh, no one in particular. He pretty much kept to himself."

"Oh, c'mon sweetie, don't be so cagey. I'm just curious about a guy who was a terrible boss to you. It's not as though I'm asking you about the Fifth Man. A glacial chill ran the length of Rick's spine in a quick tremor. A loss of breath followed. Only by a sheer act of will, born of years of experience and training, was he able to gather himself and resume a normal conversation. But things were anything but normal.

Only a handful of top CIA officials and researcher-analysts were supposed to know about the Fifth Man. He himself had heard him mentioned only a few times over the years. But now the words had slipped from the mouth of a complete civilian, his wife and beloved.

And this only a couple of weeks after her father had asked a question which presupposed a knowledge of highly confidential information.

Rick was seized with paranoia. But he had to restore his equilibrium and take control of the situation. He laughed along with Clarissa as if she had said something witty, their own inside joke. With what he hoped was an amused expression and a jocular tone, he asked, "Okay dear, where did you hear about the Fifth Man?"

Clarissa's eyes no longer showed anything but fear. Rick assumed that was because she knew she had slipped and gone too far. Her reply was a flippant one designed to gain her time to frame a better answer. "Hear about him? Isn't he a superhero in a Marvel comic book?" Recognizing her lawyer's tactic, Rick again feigned amusement by laughing in a way he hoped was convincing.

He ventured forth again. "No, but seriously sweetheart, where did you hear about the Fifth Man?" But now Clarissa dug in her heels. Dismissively she said, "I don't know. You must have mentioned him; or some name dropper might have let the expression slip at a Company cocktail party."

Clarissa knew how preposterous her response was. But it wasn't meant to deceive Rick. She knew he would not be deceived and would also not risk a confrontation with her at this time. So, in effect, her message was not "here's the truth," so much as "don't go there."

Rick would question her no further. He did not wish to ruin their evening or to risk losing the good feelings they had created over the long weekend. But a seed of doubt had been planted which could not be dislodged, but merely held in limbo until he gathered the courage to confront it head-on.

But how could he fly to the other side of the globe to meet with Carlton after such a mystifying element had been added to an ever-expanding mystery.

The answer was he would because he was a pro and that was the mission.

Chapter Eight

CARLTON

Rick hoped to limit his trip to the Crimea to four days: two travel days and two others with Carlton at his villa on the Black Sea. In their riverside condo, Rick and Clarissa orbited each other, lost in their separate preoccupations. Rick planned his interview of Carlton, consciously seeking to tamp down any element of aggressiveness. Carlton had to be handled with kid gloves. First, he had earned that courtesy; second, if pressured even in the slightest, the Russian would gently and without ostentation close down the interview. He would probably ask you to stay for dinner and perhaps to spend the night, all with a pleasant and genuinely hospitable demeanor; but the tap to his information pipeline would be tightly and irrevocably shut.

Clarissa spent her time downloading legal research and investigation results onto a CD to take back to New York with her. Her Bethesda computer was not networked with her law office's computers and that was the way she preferred it. She also ran her personal and business files off separate servers, both in Bethesda and in their New York apartment. And business and personal calls were conducted on separate cell phones.

Ever since Rick and Clarissa met she had a penchant for secrecy. But only since their evening at the Mount Vernon Inn had Rick begun to wonder if there was some surreptitious reason for her tightly compartmentalized life.

Things had been outwardly normal between them since that night, but in subtle ways only Rick would notice, Clarissa was beginning to withdraw again into that interior world having a population of one.

Rick tapped out on the coffee table some ancient Buddy Holley beat while impatiently waiting for Fasbender to pick him up. When it came to agent contact, Rick worked strictly alone; but his father, always his confidant, had warned him not to travel to a place like Crimea without an armed escort.

On that score Fasbender was as good as they came, a veteran of dangerous tours in both Kabul and Islamabad.

After his encounter with the Angleton lookalike the day of the U.N. bombing, Tom Tallifierro filed a detailed report of the incident. A tail was assigned to the man after the Agency's photo-identification lab had identified him as Walter Black, a freelance private investigator who handled odd jobs for both the Agency and the FBI, as an independent contractor. He remained under surveillance but thus far his movements had not raised any suspicions of hostile activity. Why Crowe was in front of the U.N. building that morning shortly before the explosion, was still a mystery. But Rick was heeding Booker's admonition to work forward from past events in conducting his investigation. One thing that was no mystery was that Black was the spitting image of the great counterintelligence man, James Jesus Angleton.

Fasbender pulled up in front of the condo but made no attempt to get out of his green Acura. A seasoned counterintelligence man, he lived as much by instinct as reason. It took him only one occasion together with the Tallifierros, Burns' St. Patrick's Day bash, to promptly intuit that not all was right in that mystical place near Eden where poets composed love sonnets. But he could not have known of the metastasizing doubt with which Rick had become afflicted; nor could he have perceived the slow retreat by Clarissa down the inner highway to her psychic hermitage.

A single beep of his car horn by Fasbender brought Rick out of the house carrying his bag. Their first stop was to be Langley—the Special Operations Unit, usually referred to by CIA insiders as the "Op Shop." Rick and Fasbender had an appointment for the Company's version of a makeover. The shop keeper was Mike Brandt, called "Sweeny Todd" in deference to his talent for making someone who walked into his shop radically altered when he left. Brandt was not merely a disguise artist; he was the world's preeminent master of disguise.

The two government men wearing drab suits and ties who entered the Op Shop boarded a helicopter two hours later which flew them to a nearby airfield. There they boarded a CIA jet for Athens. Greece, a fellow NATO nation, allowed a CIA unit to maintain a small airport on the outskirts of Athens for missions such as this one. From Athens, Rick and Fasbender flew nonstop on a commercial flight to Sevastopol, the Crimea's largest city located in the southwestern portion of the Peninsula, on the coast of the Black Sea.

It was not the same Richmond Tallifierro who alighted from the plane and walked stoop-shouldered through the landing gate tunnel into Sevastopol's international airport. Sweeny Todd had created in his place a shaven-headed, middle-aged man dressed in baggy slacks and an out-of-style sports jacket, over an olive-drab dress shirt adorned by a solid black bowtie. His shoes were badly scuffed wing tips with both heals unevenly worn down. A pair of granny glasses perched precariously on the tip of his nose, a fact of which he seemed oblivious. He held a microscope case tightly and close to his right side, the security of which seemed the bald man's chief interest. Every couple of minutes or so he would shift his grip on the case and fiddle with the latch, ostensibly to make sure it was still closed and locked. A gray goatee topped off his ensemble.

The passport of this odd-looking man listed his name as Antoine Dupré of Ontario, Canada. He also had a work visa for a term of up "to two months" as a microbiologist. Sevastopol Medical Center was known for being one of the finest communicable disease clinics and research centers in the world. Dr. Dupré was on a short sabbatical from the Canadian Infectious Disease Center to study the Sevastopol Clinic's experimental drug for combating cancer of the liver in its early stages.

Sweeny Todd had also disposed of Mort Fasbender. The nondescript CIA lifer had been supplanted by a fashionably dressed European linguist with a pencil-thin mustache who accompanied Dupré as his Russian interpreter. In fact, two tours of duty as an agent handler in Belarús had given Fasbender a conversational facility with Russian, which was passable. His cover name was Otto Von Kreindel of Vienna, on assignment to the United Nations, but on loan to Canada for the current project.

Like most major airports, Sevastopol International had a moving walkway to transport passengers in the direction of "Baggage Claim" and other areas of the terminal. Rick and Fasbender stood on the mobile walk as it approached a large group of limo drivers and other factotums holding signs in front of them bearing the names of arriving passengers. Standing in front of Fasbender, Rick had a view of many of the printed signs. He gazed at them indifferently since no one outside of the Op Shop would know that passengers Dupré and Von Kreindel were traveling to Crimea. Like a man taking an eye test in an ophthalmologist's office, to Rick the printing on the signs was too small and blurred to read. But as they got closer, to within about 30 feet from the end of the walkway, the letters seemed to grow larger. At about twenty feet, Rick saw the lettering clearly. He felt a tensing of his muscles and nerves. Behind the front row of sign-holders was a partially blocked sign which appeared to read, "uprés" and "on Kreindel." Obviously there were two blocked letters: "D" and "V."

The holder of the sign was a short, stocky man wearing a limo driver's uniform with the name "Yugarian" affixed to his jacket on the left side above his breast bone. An electrical impulse shot through Rick, prompting him to reach inside his jacket to feel the 9mm Glock sitting in its shoulder holster. As if they were synchronized, "Yugarian" simultaneously reached inside his jacket, withdrew a Beretta with a silencer attached and aimed it at Rick, who now feared his split-second decision to touch, but not pull, his weapon, would be fatal. "Yugarian" might be putting a bullet between Rick's eyes before he had his Glock out of its holster. As Rick drew, Yugarian fired. Rick hit the track of the moving walkway face first. But it was Fasbender's lithe and muscular body which had brought him down from behind. And as Fasbender moved Rick's six-foot three-inch frame out of his way, he pointed and shot his own weapon as the two Americans fell. Fasbender and Yugarian had fired simultaneously.

As screams of passengers and shouts of security guards and police cascaded off the tall front window of the baggage claim area, Rick, Fasbender, and Yugarian lay face down and still, with Fasbender on top of Rick.

Two airport police officers—one male and one female—got to the scene of the shootings with weapons drawn, each at about the same time as the other. They were not sure whether they would later be filing reports of a triple homicide, a lesser number of victims, or three men simply taking a bad fall. The three bodies covered an area not more than fifteen feet in circumference. The officers dropped to their knees at the sides of the men lying prostrate.

Any possibility of a fatality-free incident was instantly dispelled. A large exit wound was visible in the back of the head of one of the men. The exiting bullet had opened a jagged aperture filled with and surrounded by blood, tissue, brain fluid and particles of smashed skull.

Fasbender rose slowly under his own power, racked with anxiety over what he would find once he untangled himself from Rick's lifeless form. The two police officers spoke Russian into their radios and Fasbender heard them report "three civilians down and at least one fatality. Send backup." But there was only one fatality and Fasbender took grim satisfaction and great relief that his shot had hit Yugarian squarely in the middle of his forehead. He gently touched a spot on his own wound above his left ear and hairline. It stung and was bleeding but he knew the wound was superficial. Thankfully, Yugarian's shot was off target, probably due to Fasbender's quick diversionary action of bringing Rick to the ground.

Yugarian was dead but Rick sustained nothing worse than scrapes and bruises. Soon paramedics arrived and cleaned and bandaged Fasbender's wound.

What followed seemed to occur at Mach 2 speed. The roughly 25 square foot crime scene was cordoned off with yellow police tape. Ambulances arrived and parked adjacent to the building, visible through the floor to ceiling glass window. At least four patrol cars did the same. More than a dozen uniforms secured the area, blocked off the crime scene and handled crowd control. Several plainclothesmen interviewed Rick and Fasbender, both of whom were then cuffed.

Crime scene technicians, police photographers and inter-agency liaison officers also joined the fray. The two survivors were placed in the rear seat of a patrol car, from where they witnessed multiple, agitated conversations taking place between high ranking uniforms and various suits; and between suits and other suits. They were unable to make out what was being said. The body was left uncovered while detectives, police photographers, coroners' assistants, blood experts, ballistics specialists and crime-scene technicians searched and probed for evidence; which once retrieved was placed in small plastic bags. Soon better-dressed suits showed up in dark vans and began remonstrating to the brass and the ordinary suits. Most of the suits and brass had frequent conversations with others on their smart phones; but some texted.

After about a half-hour of frenetic activity, the two surviving

participants of the double shooting were removed from the patrol car
and placed in the back of one of the vans. Two of the better-dressed
suits accompanied them and took seats facing them on the opposite
side. Their handcuffs were removed and suddenly the van was
moving. There were no sirens or other audible noises. There were
also few stops or changes in speed. The suits stared at them in
silence. After the first twenty minutes or so, the van seemed to be
cruising down a road having the feel of the Autostrada. After about
30 minutes of smooth riding at a uniform speed, Rick was
reasonably sure they were not being taken to jail and doubted they
were still in Sevastopol.

Rick was the first to break the silence. "Do you mind telling us
where you're taking us?" Fasbender translated the question into
Russian.

"You don't need a translator. We speak English," said Suit No.
1. "We are on the Ukrainian Highway near Balaklava. Our
destination is Foroso."

For the first time since he had read Yugorian's sign, Rick felt
himself relaxing slightly. Foroso was a town at the southern tip of
the peninsula overlooking the Black Sea; and there on a seaside hill,
one of Russia's most prominent retirees lived. His name was Yuri
Putyagin and he was the former Chief of "Defense Preparedness of
the Soviet Union." To Rick he was known simply as Carlton.

"Do you know where we'll be taken in Foroso?"

"Yes."

"Can you tell us?"

"No."

"May we see your credentials?"

Both suits pulled out small leather cases from their inside
pockets and flashed their badges. The badges were emblazoned with
the Russian words for: "Crimean Special Investigations." But their
names did not appear on the badges. Simply "101" on one badge,
and "139" on the other.

After several hours of smooth riding, the van exited the

highway. During the next half-hour it made a series of turns. The roads turned bumpier and the van's speed decreased.

When Rick heard what he was sure was a ship's whistle, he ventured another question.

"Are you taking us to someone's residence?"

"You will soon see."

"Are we to be arrested?"

"Not at this time."

"Do you accept our explanation of what happened in Sevastopol; because it was the truth?"

Suit No. 2 smiled sardonically and spoke. "Not all Crimeans have passively accepted the annexation by Russia. Some are loyal to the Ukraine as an independent nation." Aside from this cryptic answer, no other explanation was offered and there were no further questions or comments. Rick allowed himself for the first time to feel his immense gratitude to Fasbender for having saved his life back at the airport. He had nothing but admiration for the lanky Nebraskan.

Rick was not sure of their ultimate destination but on the chance that they would be meeting with Carlton soon, he began mentally reviewing for about the tenth time the subject areas of greatest concern that he hoped to discuss.

The nagging worry that followed him everywhere was that his chief advisers: his father, Booker and now possibly Carlton, were old men whose better days were behind them. The positives they shared were that they were brilliant, fearless and dedicated. The negative was that their halcyon days were of a bygone era, the Cold War of the sixties and seventies. The geopolitical and technological landscape of today was so radically different from that of the 60s and 70s that they might as well have existed on different planets. Could an octogenarian like Booker fully comprehend the implications and nuances of cyberterrorism, drone warfare; suicide bombing; economic warfare and Islamic Jihad, perhaps the greatest threat to civilization? As he would soon learn, the answer was Yes.

One of the things from which he took both consolation and hope was that some special men of their era were adaptable to new realities because their character and resolve were deeply embedded. They were simple, uncynical patriots. Like Tom Tallifierro's favorite philosopher, Soren Kierkegaard, they knew that truth was subjective, not objective. Science could not prove the causes of love, courage and commitment. His father's generation grasped this reality as firmly as any which came before it; and that bestowed upon them a limitless capacity for growth.

Anyway, who else could he trust, or even respect? Burns? Crowe? The very notion was laughable. Then it dawned on him. His own sudden and rapid ascension to a position of power and responsibility had temporarily deflected him from reality. Asking himself who he could trust and rely upon wasn't even the right question; he better stop asking it to himself. The real question was, could those who relied upon him for their safety and welfare trust *him?* The very sobering answer to that question was they would soon find out.

The sudden upward movement of the van shook Rick from his reverie. It was climbing a winding, circular path. The climb took no less than fifteen minutes before it reached an even plane and then stopped.

The ground had leveled off and was now a flat tract of land, about an acre, surrounded on all sides by steep declines. A stone structure, a building whose architecture could only be described as Gothic, sat imposingly in the center of the plot. At first glance it looked like a 13th Century house of worship, replete with flying buttresses and a single steeple. But signs of residential use were apparent: a detached garage; a macadam driveway in which an SUV was parked; a front door made of pristine oak polished to a high sheen; and an estate-style sign affixed next to the front door bearing a single word painted in white ecclesiastical lettering: "Putyagin." The view from everywhere was astounding, particularly from the front garden overlooking the Black Sea.

The clime was superb: sunny, gentle breezes, temperatures in the seventies and low humidity. As Rick, Mort, and their two stolid escorts approached the front door, they could hear the whirr of central air conditioning escaping from the inside.

There was no doorbell...but instead a door knocker in the shape of a lamb. Suit No. 1 was about to knock when the door swung slowly open to present an elderly, ascetic-looking man, standing stooped over in the doorway. He had not a single hair on his head and wore a brown cassock. As he reached out to shake Rick's hand he revealed that his own right hand was a gnarled and twisted appendage ravaged by arthritis, yet his face was smooth. Before any one of the five men assembled at the doorway had an opportunity to introduce themselves, the monkish greeter, looking directly at Rick, spoke in a soft, throaty voice, "Thank you Dr. Dupré for taking the time to visit me. Why don't you and your companions come in and make yourselves comfortable.

"Vladimir, we have guests," he announced to a tall figure lurking in the hallway shadows. "Please put on a pot of tea."

Because of his still unfurrowed neck, face and brow, it was impossible to tell Carlton's age. Rick, however, was among three individuals, Burns, Booker and himself, who had access to all CIA agent files and knew that Carlton was 91.

"You must be Mr. Von Kreindel, said Carlton with a warm and friendly smile. I have heard only good things about you. It is indeed a pleasure to make your acquaintance and I hope you and I will have the opportunity to have a conversation in Russian later on."

"I would enjoy that very much," said Fasbender, as Carlton again extended the nob at the end of his right arm to shake hands. Carlton made no attempt to introduce himself. Everyone knew who he was or they wouldn't be there. He also pointedly ignored the two suits as if they were mere valets.

No one had the audacity to ask Carlton why he was dressed and groomed like an ancient Trappist monk, and Carlton offered no explanation.

After snacking on tea and wonderful French pastries, Rick and Fasbender found that their energies, which had been greatly depleted by the encounter with the would-be assassin and then the five-hour trip, were mostly restored.

Carlton orchestrated the conversation as they ate, confining it to small talk about the climate, local customs, trade, fishing and the flora and fauna of southern Crimea. The man was a talking National Geographic Magazine. But he never rambled or repeated himself, and was courteous and attentive when either of the two Americans interjected a comment. Yet he yielded not even the slightest degree of control over the conversation.

As if on a NASA flight schedule, he immediately changed the tenor of the proceedings as soon as Vladimir appeared from nowhere to wheel the refreshments tray out of the room. Without moving his body, but turning his head almost imperceptibly toward the two suits, Carlton spoke to them for the first time, "Would you gentlemen please excuse us?" Carlton gave no sign of going anywhere, so the two men rose at once and not only walked out of the room but also vacated the premises. Rick assumed they would wait in the van until the meeting was over.

The three remaining men sat in comfortable arm chairs around an oversized coffee table which (Rick surmised) did double-duty as a conference table.

Carlton was quiet, but while he was probably too polite to say so, the enigmatic expression on his face seemed to be signaling that there would be no more small talk and it was time for them to state their business.

If there were any semblance of normalcy in their lives, Rick might have expressed his condolences to Carlton for the loss of his old friend Fred Reitenhauser; but among spies there were definite boundaries beyond which one did not go. Any allusion to a relationship between a covert operative and his case officer would be a serious breach of the unwritten code which bound them all.

After straightening his posture in the comfortable arm chair,

Rick spoke first. "Komisar Putyagin, the Western world is faced with a dual challenge. First, the proliferation of Islamic Jihad is out of control. Its terrorism and brutality are no longer mainly centered in Afghanistan and Pakistan. The Middle East and large parts of Africa are now ablaze with war; in Iraq, Syria, the Sudan, Somalia, Nigeria, Libya, Gaza and Yemen; plus, growing acts of terrorism inspired by ISIS in Europe and America. Second, Russia's relentless encroachments in Northeastern Ukraine are alarming. NATO is deeply concerned that Putin's offensive operations pose a threat to the entire Ukraine, the Balkans, Poland and the Baltic states.

In the wake of the attack upon the United Nations Headquarters, our intelligence services have focused like never before on identifying the core participants in the various plots and conspiracies behind the hostilities.

We now believe that the widespread civil unrest and insurrection, rooted in religious, tribal and ethnic hatreds have been abetted by a powerful conspiracy deeply entrenched in Europe, the U.S. and Canada.

We also have empirical evidence that the origins of the conspiracy date back to the middle of the Twentieth Century. Our best evidence reveals that the conspiracy is a traditional covert operation conducted with the expert espionage and counterespionage tradecraft practiced by Great Britain, the U.S. and Russia.

The top leaders of my country believe that the emphasis by the CIA on paramilitary operations may have caused it to take its eye off the ball. Our best minds have concluded that the conspiracy can only be countered effectively by espionage and counterespionage of the highest grade. But we are in need of the type of information and advice that know no time restriction, that are not limited in their historical reach or scope. That is why we are here today. Our superiors in Washington have tasked us with meeting with you and becoming as informed as possible in the areas I have mentioned. That is our mission and I hope you will be able to help us."

Rick sat back and checked for any body language by Carlton

which would reveal his reaction to what had just been said. But Carlton was as inscrutable as a Tibetan Buddhist. He simply sat impassively. He uttered not a word for a good two minutes, all the while with the traces of a smile on his face.

Finally, he spoke. "You know, during the Nazi War Crimes Trial in 1945 and 46, my great American friend and I were young officers on the investigative staff of the Allies' chief prosecutor, Robert H. Jackson. Among the accused were the notorious Göring, Borrman, Hess, Jodl, Kaltenbrunner and von Ribbentrop. My friend, Fred, and I were brimming with curiosity about how these men who had carried out the greatest genocide known to man, would look and how they would act."

"Did evil have a special smell? Would the Nazis have a murderous look in their eyes? Would they carry themselves in a contemptuous or threatening manner? Would they seem dangerous?"

"We were quite disappointed to observe none of those things. These mass murderers looked pretty much like anyone else. If we knew nothing about them and were told that they were a group of low-level government clerks, we would not have been surprised when we saw them. Some were balding; others wore glasses or hearing aids; still others were overweight and some were skinny. In short, as a group they seemed ordinary. On the whole they personified Hanna Arendt's description of the "banality of evil.""

"Before the war, when I was a Russian diplomat's son living in London and attending Cambridge, I became friendly with a charming fellow named Kim Philby. Kim was a people magnet. His combination of good looks, brains, wit, and an engaging personality were so attractive that almost everyone wanted to be his friend."

"During World War II he was effective in exposing Nazi spies in Great Britain and elsewhere. But from the first day he served as a British intelligence officer until the day he defected to the Soviet Union almost thirty years later, he was a double agent whose true loyalty was to the U.S.S.R. CIA and British agents would refer to him and his fellow defectors, Burgess, Maclean and Blunt, as the "Red Four."

"At least in the case of Philby, the name was well-deserved. He joined the Communist Party in 1933 and never looked back, while building a flawless reputation in the British Secret Service as a skilled intelligence officer and a true patriot. He betrayed his country continuously for more than two decades. Not a single written communication between Churchill and Roosevelt during the war, related to strategy, materiél or tactics, eluded Philby's grasp. Copies of all were turned over to his Soviet handlers."

"So adept was Philby at deception that his two close friends and fellow operatives, Elliott and Angleton, never suspected a thing until the mid-fifties. Hundreds of potential defectors behind the Iron Curtain and confederates in anti-Soviet causes lost their lives because of Philby's betrayals."

"Think about this as you embark upon your mission. And just think about how many times you read in the newspapers of people who encountered serial killers and described them as seeming 'normal' or 'ordinary'. I use the example of Philby to demonstrate that evil often wears a mask. And the most effective masks are those that disguise a bad man from himself, that allow him to rationalize stealing another's life or freedom as a necessary evil."

Carlton stopped at that point, perhaps to let his message sink in. This gave Rick an opportunity to move the discussion further along. "Komisar Putyagin, your reference to Philby is a particularly apt one because there are signs of deeply embedded moles working for our enemies, who were either instructed or inspired by Philby."

Carlton chuckled softly before responding. "Indeed, as many as there were who referred to the double agents as the 'Red Four', there were others who chose instead the appellation, 'The Cambridge Five', even though the identity of the Fifth Man has never been established."

"Well, there must have come a time, Komisar, when you learned that Philby was a double agent?"

"Oh yes, I found out about him as you Americans like to say, through the grape vine. It was in 1958 or 1959 when Moscow Central was preparing to put Francis Gary Powers, the American U-2 pilot, on trial as a spy. As Director of Soviet Defense Preparedness, the massive flow of documents across my desk was more than I could handle. I had to hire two additional clerks to keep from being drowned in a sea of paper."

"Quite by accident one day, one of the clerks picked up off the floor a bound report entitled "A History of the Use of U-2s for spy missions on the Soviet Union," by T. J. Stanley, which was one of Philby's several cover names. I had a "need to know" the contents because of the position I held, so I skimmed through it. It chronicled every spy mission Powers ever performed, more than thirty of them, mostly against the U.S.S.R. I was astounded that Philby was able to collect such a treasure trove of top secret intelligence. So I made some inquiries and found out that Philby had been a secret NKPD agent since 1938."

"I managed to expose Philby to a CIA colleague, who in turn told Angleton. But neither the United States nor Great Britain could prosecute him, for lack of hard evidence. The Americans could not reveal that I was the source of the information, so the whole incident just died. After Philby defected to the U.S.S.R. in 1963, we resumed our relationship, first begun at Cambridge."

"You mentioned the fact that the identity of the so-called 'Fifth Man' has never been established," said Rick, "but our investigation has unearthed some pretty convincing data pointing to the Fifth Man as the first in a line of successors to Philby, each of whom was implanted as a mole somewhere in the U.S.'s matrix of seventeen intelligence agencies. We're hopeful that you might be able to give us the benefit of your wisdom as to the direction the investigation should take in attempting to find the moles."

"Well, Dr. Duprés, there is much information available to you. You will have to do a lot of digging."

"I understand that," said Rick, "but the situation is urgent. We're hoping you can point us in the right direction."

Carlton, who almost never answered a question directly, appeared to mull this one over, folding his arms and gazing at the ceiling.

"Dr., I know you are a man of science, not the law, but in England, as well as in America, every corporate charter must be filed with the local governmental authority. In America that means the state where the corporation has its main office. You might wish to check the corporate records in New York and the District of Columbia for a company named Harp Affiliates, Inc."

"I see; what type of business are they in?"

"One can only speculate about that Dr. Duprés. But as you do what your generation of professionals calls 'due diligence', much will be revealed."

With that cryptic remark, Carlton picked up the phone on the lamp table beside him and pressed the intercom button.

"Vladimir, when can we expect dinner to be ready? In about fifteen minutes? Excellent. Gentlemen let us repair to the library for cocktails."

Rick and Fasbender compliantly followed Carlton down a long hall to a spacious interior room having a pleasant smell of furniture polish combined with a musty scent. There they were treated to a stunning sight. The room was as perfectly round as a carousel and from the floor to a twenty-foot-high ceiling stood polished oak book shelves of exquisite grain, filled with mostly leather-bound volumns. At two locations stood shelf ladders on wheels. The furniture of the library-in-the-round was either Chippendale or Queen Anne, comprised of plush upholstered arm chairs, a maple coffee table and two mahogany desks. The carpet was oriental and looked expensive, but neither visitor was knowledgeable enough to know much more than that. The array of books was remarkable. Yes, there were works by Tolstoy, Dostoyevsky, Pushkin, Solzhenitsyn and Pasternak—not unexpected for a learned Russian man. But that was only the beginning. There were also leather-bound works by Flaubert,

Cervantes, Dickens, Balzac, Proust, Zola, Ibsen, Milton, Homer, Plutarch, Thackeray, Austin, Shakespeare, Dante, Fielding and Swift. And so as not to slight the Americans, there were Faulkners, Hawthornes, Twains, Conrads, Hemingways, Fitzgeralds, Eugene O'Neills, Arthur Millers, and on and on. Mixed in with the classics were books by le Carré, Mickey Spillane, and Joseph Heller's "Catch 22."

In a grouping were Ian Fleming's James Bond novels. There were sections with nothing but books on philosophy, others with only history, and still others filled exclusively with poetry. And there were physics, art, anthropology, archeology, mathematics and astronomy books as well.

Rick's thoughts drifted to Clarissa and how sublimely happy it would make her to have a library like this one. But just as quickly he was yanked back from his day dream to the sobering reality of the moment. Whether they knew it or not—and most persons could not—countless more American lives might be lost if Rick was unable to learn the identity of the Fifth Man and his deadly descendants. The magnificent books which now surrounded Rick held the answers to many of mankind's most profound questions. But not one of those thousands of titles could tell him what Harp Affiliates was and how it could lead him to the deeply-entrenched miscreants who with delight, sought to cause pain, death, destruction and grief. It was time to go home and get to work.

Chapter Nine

HARP

After their experience in Sevastopol, Richmond Tallifierro and Morton Fasbender were anxious to get out of the Crimea, fly home and shed their cover identities. But because it was past 10:00 p.m. before they finished their dinner of Château Briand with baked Alaska for dessert, followed by brandy in the library, they accepted Carlton's gracious invitation to spend the night. Following a breakfast of Eggs Benedict and rich Columbian coffee the next morning, the two suits, who Rick hoped were fed, drove them back to Sevastopol where they reversed their journey into Crimea by flying from Sevastopol to Athens, to Washington, DC and to Langley.

On the nonstop flight from Greece to Washington, Rick did a mental inventory of the plusses and minuses of the mission.

Certainly the attempt on their lives was not exactly the high point, though in the long run it might provide valuable clues.

The interview of Carlton was about as instructive as they could have hoped for. The mere fact that Carlton had discoursed on

Philby, the Fifth Man and Harp Affiliates was itself confirmation that they were on the right track.

Rick had been warned that Carlton was the master of the oblique and had discounted that going in. Nevertheless, the disclosure of Harp Affiliates, Inc. was undoubtedly a good starting place, or else he would not have revealed it. Harp would be the jumping off point of the next phase of the investigation, or perhaps "excavation" was a more descriptive word. But first Rick chastised himself for not having tapped all of the known data at his disposal; by his failing to first meet with the Director of National Intelligence, James R. Clapper, whose umbrella organization monitored and integrated the activities of the seventeen United States intelligence agencies. Confronted with the failures of the CIA and FBI to share critical intelligence internally and with each other prior to 9/11, Congress created during the George W. Bush administration, the office of the National Director of Intelligence, to manage the integration of the various components of the U.S. intelligence community.

Lastly, Rick vowed to himself never to forget Carlton's admonition on the banality of evil, that the most innocuous appearing individual could be a dangerous traitor and anarchist.

Arriving home on a Thursday, Rick was able to grab a shuttle to New York. He called Clarissa from his cell phone before takeoff. She excitedly told him not to eat anything because she would prepare a special dinner. He decided not to tell her about what had happened in Sevastopol because it would only upset her. Of course, he couldn't tell her about Carlton either. In fact, he really could tell her nothing about what had happened between the moment Fasbender picked him up in front of their Bethesda condo and the phone call he had just placed. Such time warps were everyday occurrences in covert intelligence work and did not bother him at all. What did bother him greatly was that he may have another reason for withholding information from Clarissa, one that had the potential to shake their world. He wouldn't worry about that tonight. Now he just missed his wife and couldn't wait to get home.

Clarissa had a surprise for Rick when he walked through the front door to their apartment. Each of her hands held a newborn kitten, one white and one black. On her face, Clarissa wore a smile of joy mixed with mischief; her laughter carried a lilt of happiness.

"Say 'hi' sweetheart, to Cato and Plato, our new sub-tenants." To describe Rick's reaction as surprised would have been a gross understatement. "Flabbergasted," or "incredulous" hit much closer to the mark. As long as he had known her, Clarissa had voiced strong opposition to the ownership of domestic pets. "They require too much time to care for; they often create crippling dependency upon them by the humans in the house; and they make traveling more difficult."

Cynthia Torres' cat had just given birth to a litter of kittens and Torres offered two of them to Clarissa. Clarissa was at first hesitant to accept them but enthusiastically said yes when Torres offered to take care of them when Clarissa and Rick were out of town.

Two of the things that had always fascinated Rick about Clarissa were her mercurial nature and her unpredictability. Lately, however, those very traits which had made her so attractive to Rick had become a source of great concern.

After an evening of relaxation with Clarissa, Cato and Plato, Rick was up early the next morning to shuttle back to Washington for his appointment with Director Clapper at the Office of the Director of National Intelligence (O.D.N.I.).

At 9:30 a.m. Rick was exhibiting his credentials to a security guard in the lobby of the O.D.N.I. and by 9:35 a.m. he had cleared the metal detector. As a young veteran of Washington customs and mores, he was not surprised when the O.D.N.I. receptionist told him he would be meeting with the Director's Chief Deputy rather than the Director himself.

Seeing the young Deputy Director behind his desk in his ample office with a view of the Washington Monument, struck a chord of recognition in Rick. Out of context, however, Rick needed about thirty seconds to place him. Kyle Collins, the former Chief

Administrative Aide to Congressman Mark Scherzer, certainly was enjoying fancier digs than he had on Capitol Hill.

With the vast number of tasks to be completed by Rick and Fasbender, who to Rick was now simply "Mort," he had no time for small talk.

"Good morning Mr. Tallifierro; it's always a pleasure to see you."

"And I you, Mr. Collins. Let me get right to the point. I need whatever information this office has on a corporation named Harp Affiliates, Inc."

Collins' manner was officious, just as it had been in Scherzer's office. "I'm sure you understand, Mr. Tallifierro, that any inter-agency request for information must be cleared by the Director, who right now is in Brazil."

Rick was having none of it. Without further talk, he pulled from his pocket a letter on White House stationery bearing the Presidential Seal and the President's original signature, directing the entire Executive Branch of the government to immediately give Richmond Tallifierro, "Counterintelligence Director of the United States," whatever he asked for. Rick thought the new title conferred by the President was a nice touch. With a resentful though somewhat chastened expression on his face, Collins began punching keys on his computer. After about a minute of entering PINS, codes and passwords, Collins grudgingly turned toward Rick and spoke. "Harp Affiliates, Inc., a Delaware Corporation, Certificate of Incorporation filed March 9, 1963, Incorporators, Quentin Quarles and Spencer Pauley; Purposes of incorporation: to conduct international currency and commerce transactions."

"Thank you, and now print for me whatever you have on your computer for Harp Affiliates." Collins' body language said he was about to protest but then thought better of it. He compliantly pressed the print button and handed the single page of information to Rick.

"Do you have an index for publications on file?"

"Yes, that too is in our computer system."

"Good, print that too."

Collins had lost his condescending attitude. He meekly complied.

"Now, Mr. Collins, Deputy Director of Counterintelligence, Morton Fasbender, will be joining me here to review this index. Please direct me to a room where the two of us can have some privacy and quiet."

Mort Fasbender arrived at O.D.N.I. at 10:00 a.m. sharp, the pre-appointed time. The O.D.N.I. was the coordinating body for seventeen intelligence agencies. It had in its computer hard drive a list of 2431 publications on intelligence topics with the name of the author or authors, the year of publication, the number of pages and a few descriptive words about each one. Many were classified "NOFORN." Some were classified as "restricted" documents and others "top secret." Just as many were "unclassified" or "declassified." In their windowless conference room, Rick and Mort divided the 34 page print out between them—Rick keeping pages 1 through 17—and Mort the rest. Each of them used a yellow highlighter to note those publications of possible relevance, and a green highlighter to designate publications of high interest.

After perusing the list of publications for an hour and a half, each had marked multiple "possibles." Rick had highlighted only two "of high interest," and Mort three. Before exchanging pages, Rick sighed wearily. "You know what Mort, a team composed of you, me and a few house investigators just isn't going to cut it. We need to beef up our team with some hardworking and smart heavyweights. We can no longer afford to sacrifice staffing for secrecy. We face a mammoth project here and we might not have much time to get it done."

"Anyone in particular in mind?"

"So far I'm thinking of two possible additions. My father did some research on his own on a fellow who was with Porter Crowe on the morning of the U.N. bombing, under some strange circumstances. I had the FBI investigate the contact/incident and their report cleared it as innocent. It turns out the guy's name is Walter Black and to Intelligence vets of my dad's generation, he is a dead-ringer for the famous James Jesus Angleton. This piqued my curiosity so I did some checking of my own. It turns out that Black was an associate of Crowe and the latter handpicked him for his official U.N. bombing investigation, as its Executive Director. After a month on the job, Black abruptly quit his post, citing personal family issues. But my sources tell me Black considered Crowe an empty suit and an incompetent, whose investigation was destined to crash and burn. I got a hold of Black's résumé from Personnel and was greatly impressed. As a young CIA agent he infiltrated into Afghanistan in the late Fall of 2001 with Army Special Ops. He recruited a team of about a half-dozen local tribesmen, who hated the Taliban, to spy for us and identify Al Qaeda units. His unit fed our paramilitary guys vital information on Al Qaeda's locations all the way to Pakistan. He did two tours in Afghanistan and one in Iraq. Back at Langley he shed his agent-handler profile and was sent into deep cover for special investigations. Since he quit Crowe's team, he has been looking to land a new job. He could be just right for us as a planner, analyst and someone with an inside track on the Crowe investigation.

"Sounds good. Who's your second prospect?"

"A dynamite mid-thirtyish criminal prosecutor with the U.S. Attorney's office, Eastern District, New York, named Cynthia Torres, appointed six months ago as chief of their anti-terrorism task force."

"With a position like that why would she want to leave to join us?"

"First, Mort, because she wouldn't be leaving. She'd simply take a leave of absence at the request of the President for the duration of the investigation, because it's her patriotic duty. Without her knowledge I've already started her security check on an expedited basis. I intend to pitch her over the weekend. We also need to add a couple of researchers and two security guys. Those I'll select from our counterintelligence section."

A smile of pleasure crossed Mort's face. "Rick, as an intelligence pro one can get jaded. But with this project, I can't help but get excited."

"Me too buddy," said Rick.

It was now Fasbender's turn to deal with the arrogant Kyle Collins. So he marched into his office with a list of the five publications they agreed were of "high interest."

1. The History of the OSS and CIA
   by James Jesus Angleton and William E. Colby

2. The Cambridge Five
   by Richard Helms

3. The Art of Crafting a Cover Organization
   by Allen Dulles

4. The Trial of Alger Hiss
   by Roy Cohn

5. Treachery: The Stories of Robert Hansen and Aldrich Ames
   by Brent Bozell and William F. Buckley, Jr.

Collins at first resisted the demand upon the grounds that O.D.N.I. did not have the materials; and they would have to get them from the CIA Library themselves. And, of course, they could have done that, but by this time Rick was fed up with Collins. He had Mort show Collins the publications' index number/letters combo, which indicated that O.D.N.I. had several copies of each. Collins was sent to fetch them.

Rick decided to spend the rest of the day back at Langley reading the one thousand page, "The History of the OSS and CIA." In his office, he shed his jacket and tie, told his secretary no calls and no visitors, put a yellow legal pad on his desk and several roller-tip pens next to it, and started reading.

Rick was already familiar with much of the contents of the report. His main focus now was Philby and his confederates. The portion of the report dealing with the Cambridge Five was of great interest to him. But the speculation as to the identity of the Fifth Man in this allegedly definitive history was no more revealing than what Rick already knew. It did, however, provide a couple of clues, even though the tome had been declassified. For one, a few sentences in the lengthy section on Philby were intriguing: "Philby's tentacles reached far. MI-6, resting on its blind delusions about its fair haired boy, would routinely dismiss the notion that there might be a conspiracy. In fact, Philby was believed by MI-5 to be the head of a spy dynasty which reached laterally to Burgess, Maclean and Blunt; and vertically to Philby's subordinates."

"Just tantalizing enough," Rick thought, "to try to pick up Philby's trail."

He had a dogged intuition that somehow Harp Affiliates was the common thread leading to the identities of Philby's successors in treachery, including the Fifth Man.

A second clue was contained in a very general discussion of Philby's business associates. "Philby was known to have extensive business dealings in the early 60s with Foster Wright, the president of the United States European Trade and Currency Council." Foster Wright... Why did that name seem familiar? It would come to him, but probably not until later.

Rick checked the book's thirty-page index. No other mention of Foster Wright. He trolled his own confidential website but again nothing on a Foster Wright. Google and Wikipedia searches also came up dry.

He decided to try a different approach. He would seek to expand the scope of the network of Philby's friends and associates. Philby's two closest friends and fellow intelligence operatives were the Brit, Nicholas Elliott, and the American, James J. Angleton. Angleton was co-author of the report, and had a secrecy obsession. He was not likely to have allowed anything revealing about himself to go into the history. Rick flipped to the section on Elliott. He was a different story. No one was closer to Philby than Elliott. Philby was almost like a brother. He was his best buddy, his partner in mischievous pranks, his mentor, and his confidant. Each man ran his own separate network of agents with MI-6, but Elliott thought that for almost two decades they had helped each other by sharing their secrets. In the end it was clear that Elliott had shared everything with Philby but Philby had shared nothing of value with him.

MI-5 was on to Philby by the late 40s, but a lack of hard evidence combined with the intransigence of MI-6, including the steadfast loyalty by Elliott to his friend, prevented them from making a prosecutable case. Neither Elliott nor Angleton could bring himself to believe that their charming, brilliant and kind friend was a traitor.

But by slow accretion, the body of evidence against Philby grew until it became so indisputable that even Elliott came to accept Philby's guilt. This fact shook Elliott's world, undercut his self-confidence and smashed to pieces his faith and trust in the underpinnings of his profession. He came to doubt the integrity of his colleagues. His love of Philby turned to hate. But, Elliott could construct a façade as well as anyone; and in January of 1963 he accepted the assignment from the Chief of British Intelligence to meet with Philby in Beirut, interrogate him and expose him. Over a several day period, against Philby's strong resistance, Elliott extracted a partial confession from him, admitting his own guilt but exposing almost nothing about his spy network or the identity of other Brits who were complicit.

Philby also revealed nothing about his American co-conspirators. He had spent three years in Washington, DC—from 1949 through 1951—working with Angleton, but all the while betraying him.

But, Elliott was tenacious. The last time he and Philby met before the latter defected to the Soviet Union, Elliott came armed with a list of twelve men suspected by the British Secret Service of being Soviet Spies. Naturally, Philby's three fellow defectors—Guy Burgess, Donald Maclean and Anthony Blunt—were on there, but so were three others from the Cambridge set, any one of whom could have been the Fifth Man. They were John Cairncross, Tim Milne (Philby's old school chum) and Guy Liddell, who was forced out of MI-5 under a cloud of suspicion. Tomás Harris, Philby's friend and the host of many of the set's parties, was also on the list. So, seven on the list were known; five unknown. But any one of nine on the list could have been the Fifth Man. Philby denied the guilt of everyone on the list.

Foster Wright's name suddenly raced across Rick's mind again and as it did, some instinct caused him to pick up the printout on Harp Affiliates and read it for about the fourth time. His gaze came to rest on the purposes of incorporation: "to conduct international currency and commerce transactions." What did the Angleton-Colby book say about Foster Wright? Oh yes, a member of "The President of the United States' European Trade and Currency Council." Mere coincidence? Not likely. But, then again, other than Carlton's say so, what did they really have tying Philby to Harp Affiliates? There was at best, a tenuous connection between Foster Wright and Harp. But, the name of the first incorporator, Quentin Quarles, was also suspicious, though Rick could not really say why. And the date of incorporation, March 9, 1963, was less than a month after Philby defected to the U.S.S.R.

Quentin Quarles. Initials QQ. Unusual to say the least. But wait, didn't Booker tell him about the man who called himself "Q?" That he was supposedly the founder of the fictitious Coriolanus, and believed to be a former rogue chief of the CIA station in Munich in the 60s through the early 80s? And Q, said Booker at first, spawned the violent A.O.R. So what if Booker now says those two legions of perdition never existed? That is of little importance from an evidentiary standpoint in the spy business, where for instance a wife sometimes never learns her husband's real name. It was still another connection! He felt himself passing the point where the mounting circumstances could still be attributed to coincidence.

Rick sat back and began trying to convince himself that the very fact that Carlton had set them on the path of Harp Affiliates established a nexus between Philby and Q as Philby's true successor, and as a terrorist. Could Q have been the Fifth Man? Was Q Foster Wright? Was he Philby's successor? "Reality Check, Rick!"

It was all weak circumstantial evidence. He still had nothing of substance linking Q and/or Harp Affiliates, to Philby and/or the Cambridge Five. But the mounting evidence was still worthy of aggressively chasing it to wherever it led.

To assuage his frustration, Rick began casually flipping the pages of "The History of the CIA and OSS." He was hardly focusing on any of the words. But suddenly he did a double take and flipped back a page after a few words caught his attention. "What was Philby's full name? His first name was not Kim. That was just a nickname his father had bestowed upon him, after a character in a Kipling novel. His actual name was Harold: Harold Adrian Russell Philby."

Rick wrote out the full name on his pad and then printed Philby's initials, H.A.R.P.

"So there it is," Rick murmured to himself as a wave of new excitement flowed through him.

Chapter Ten

ANGLETON

Rick had enough self-awareness to realize that now when he and Clarissa were together, there were two distinct sides to him. One was a man who ardently loved and respected his wife. The other— the hidden side—was a man beset with doubts and suspicions, which began with her remark on "The Fifth Man," and was followed by her frequent flights to the hidden corners of her being.

It often seemed like there were four (not two) people in the room—a product of their dual psychological make-ups.

But the far bigger question than that was whether Clarissa's pathology signified more than just a psycho-emotional issue. But when Rick felt his mind headed down that road he would pull himself back with a stern self-reprimand. "Paranoid" and "delusional" were among the accusations he hurled at himself.

However, self-disapprobation was not working this particular night. It was too soon after the latest troubling incident, one which took place that evening at the dinner table. It had been a lighthearted evening up to that point. Both of them were at the top of their witty remarks game as they carried on a mildly teasing banter, full of flirtation. Eventually, however, they each tired of the game and lapsed into a relaxed and pleasant silence. Rick felt it was the right time to bring up a subject he had been avoiding for the past week. "Clarissa, I have to violate my code by telling you something tonight about work, because I feel it concerns you as well."

"Let me guess," said Clarissa, "the National Security Adviser is predicting nuclear winter for the entire Eastern seaboard."

"No it's not quite that serious," said Rick, after an appropriate chuckle. "I just wanted you to know, because the two of you are close friends, that I have asked Cynthia to join one of my investigative teams, and she has accepted."

This time Clarissa offered no sardonic remark. "Cynthia Torres?" she asked with obvious incredulity. "Why would you do that?"

Rick caught the acerbic tone to her question and knew he was treading on dangerous ground.

"Oh, I considered her to be highly qualified for the position, just what we need in fact, so I made the pitch."

"You just made the pitch, did you? I'm surprised that she let herself catch it."

This time he heard more than a slight sourness. Her tone was angry, as were her eyes.

"I can see this news is upsetting you. I'm sorry. But I have to do my job, and that means doing what I think is best for the country, and for us."

"For us? Don't make me laugh. 'Us' is plural and if you cared so much about us, you would have discussed this with me first." Rick tried to formulate an appropriate apology which would also convey to her that he truly believed his decision was the right one. But before he could even open his mouth, Clarissa pivoted, showed him her back, marched off to the bedroom and slammed the door.

Richmond Tallifierro always knew that making a life-long career out of something his father had chosen to do only part-time would be hard. What he had underestimated was just how intrusive his profession would be into every part of his life. The next day, as he carefully prepared his request to the White House to grant him unfettered access to Angleton's top secret files, notes and memoranda, he took a brief personal inventory. Other than Mort Fasbender, he had no friends. Anything friends might want to talk about had been preempted by subjects he couldn't discuss. He had no time anyway. He was working seven days a week, 14 hours a day. He couldn't discuss his investigation with Burns. (Burns didn't even know about it, and he didn't trust him anyway.) And his marriage? He wouldn't even go there right now. His sense of isolation was almost complete.

In his isolation, he sat outside the Oval Office rehearsing how he would summarize his findings thus far and how he would frame his plea to fully access all Angleton's papers, even those which were highly restricted.

A half-hour later he emerged from the Oval Office after an intense meeting with the President and the National Security Adviser. In his brief case was the presidential order to all government departments, bureaus and agencies to "render no hindrance to Richmond Tallifierro or his deputy, Morton Fasbender, in gaining access to the official papers and records of the United States of America, including those which were sealed."

If Rick were not so preoccupied, he might have appreciated what had just happened. He had been named, in effect, Inquisitor-in-Chief, with full power to subpoena and/or interrogate the entire United States government, save the President himself.

Years later when he would think back on the extraordinary power he had been granted, Rick never for a minute believed that the power was commensurate with his ability. Only a fool would think he had earned it on merit. He knew that he just happened to be the right man at the right place and time. He ascended to power at a time when the CIA and FBI were rife with knaves and underachievers. He was the right age, had the right pedigree, the right promoters (Booker and Reitenhauser) and a clean, impressive résumé. He was perceived by the White House as being honest, apolitical, independent and savvy. Those things he was. He also had Booker's endorsement, which was more important than anything except for one thing. And that thing was that the government of the United States was in a state of panic over the fact that it had misidentified its enemies badly since 9/11 and even before, by being hoodwinked into thinking that its greatest foes were well-organized, well-manned and well-armed paramilitary groups. In fact, all of the attacks and terrorist acts were orchestrated from a command center comprised of no more than a few diabolically clever operators—buried deep.

Despite his orders from the President, his celebrity at the CIA and the sense of urgency surrounding his mission, at Langley, Rick still had to be escorted by two scary-looking security types. They led him to a private elevator, well-hidden behind multiple code-entry doors. Three floors below ground level the elevator deposited them into a long, empty corridor with lighting conditions he imagined must have been inspired by Abu Graib Prison.

The CIA Archives to which Rick and his two somber escorts were granted admission after a long and silent walk, carried the highest level of restriction imposed by the U. S. Government. Only those carrying orders from the President were permitted in the Archives. But once inside, there were no obvious restrictions. Rick was left alone and ostensibly free to look at anything he wanted. Of course, his pen, camera and cellphone had been confiscated and there were elevated cameras covering every square inch of the massive floor space. There were no computers, copying machines, microfiche viewers, pens, pencils or paper upon which to take notes. Rick, however, by training and lots of practice, had acquired the skill of looking at a written document or visual aid with total concentration, committing the critical parts to memory and then later reducing them to writing or to a drawing. His re-creation might not be word-perfect but it always contained everything which was important.

He spent about an hour perusing the indices to the internal reports; and published books and articles authored by Angleton. None of them seemed promising for the three central inquiries of his search:

1. Did Philby have a successor?

2. If so who was he?; and

3. Will the answers to questions "1" and "2" shed any light on the identity of the current mole or moles?

The official minutes and unofficial memoranda of Angleton's meetings were equally of no help.

Having eliminated the obvious possible sources of information, he started pulling down from the shelves the materials which he believed were most likely to yield valuable data. They consisted of more than one hundred standard size loose-leaf notebooks, each bearing the same singular label printed with a black marker: "J.J.A."; and with the year next to it. They went back only to 1960 and ran consecutively to 1976, Angleton's last year at the Agency. For the year 1960 there was only one full loose-leaf notebook; for 1976 there was also one but it was only about twenty percent full: "J.J.A. '76." For 1963 there were fourteen notebooks; and for 1964, seventeen. There were no less than five books for each year in the period 1965 through 1975. The early 70s were no surprise given the Watergate crisis from 1972 through 1976; nor was the period 1965 through 1970, the most intensive period of combat operations conducted by the U.S. in the Vietnam War.

It was interesting that for 1963, the year of Philby's defection, there were fourteen books. Rick decided to review 1963 first.

Angleton's notebooks were written with black ink in neat cursive, using a fountain pen. There were few cross-outs and they read like a novel. Angleton was privy to Elliott's final interviews with Philby. His use of adjectives to describe the interviews and subsequent defection, such as "tragic" and "shocking," betrayed his strong emotional connection to the events.

During Philby's time in Washington, Angleton had often lunched and dined with him. They had known each other well for almost fifteen years, including during Angleton's time in London with the OSS, before his transfer to Italy in early 1945. One of the more capable of men himself, Angleton was still in awe of Philby's intelligence and magnetism. Once Philby lost his security clearances and MI-5 was hot on his trail, Angleton was shaken. When Philby defected, he was profoundly affected by the finality of the event. If Philby could be a traitor anyone could, thought Angleton; and the rest of his career was noted for his conviction that no one—no matter high up and highly regarded—was above suspicion.

Much of the content of Angleton's multiple journals for 1963 and 1964 concerned his theories on anti-American conspiracies to undermine the government, carried on by disparate groups and individuals, including higher-ups in allegedly friendly nations. It also implicated, implausibly, former heads of U.S. and British Intelligence. Rick spent an inordinate amount of time on his first day in the Archives reading vast amounts of well written prose, of little value.

On his second day in the Archives, however, he came across a list of entities suspected by Angleton of being subversive organizations. There were scores of names on the list—some as unlikely as the International Red Cross and UNESCO—but others that Rick himself might have listed. It was on page "6" of the list that there appeared a single entry: "HARP AFFILIATES, INC., President: Quentin Quarles; Vice President and Secretary: Spencer Pauley." An asterisk appeared next to "Quarles," directing the reader to the bottom of the page where there appeared an intriguing footnote: "a/k/a Foster Wright."

He was beginning to chip away at the edges of the conspiracy. It was now highly likely that Foster Wright, a Philby associate, a/k/a "Quentin Quarles," and likely also known as "Q," was a key player. But the challenge was to flesh out the cabal and carry it forward to the present day. It wasn't even known for sure if Wright was still alive.

Rick lifted his head from the journal on the table in front of him and began to do some soul searching. Since Kyle Collins had produced for him the report on Harp Affiliates back at the O.D.N.I., he had been mired in a clear state of denial—contrary to his training and instincts as an intelligence pro. It was time to end the denial lest it become an insurmountable obstacle to his investigation and to his own emotional stability. He looked down at page 6 and silently formed the words appearing after "Quentin Quarles": "Vice President and Secretary: 'Spencer Pauley'."

Of course, it could have been pure coincidence that Rick's father-in-law's name was Paul Spence, but strong intuition told him it was not.

This was a depressing note upon which to end the second day in the Angleton Archives. But it was late anyway and he and Clarissa were entertaining Cynthia Torres and a date at their home in Bethesda, so he headed home under a cloud of gloom. At least Clarissa had come around to the fact that Torres was now one of her husband's investigators. The evening turned out to be a pleasant one and was an emotional escape for Rick from the onerous task of searching under rocks.

Day three in the Archives began at 8:30 a.m. Rick was able to grab a cup of bad coffee from the machine in the corridor before getting down to work. He was going to need it; he had a long day ahead of him. So far he had completed 1963 and '64 and hoped to make some real headway that day through the Vietnam War years.

He began Angleton's journal for 1965 with a clear head and renewed sense of purpose, anxious to build on what he had learned up to that point. Unfortunately, both 1965 and 1966 covered a single topic: the "Phoenix Project." It had been a CIA venture to identify and destroy the governmental infrastructure of the Viet Cong, by information obtained from paid local nationals living in Cong-controlled regions. In two days of reading Angleton's voluminous account of Operation Phoenix, Rick found not a single mention of

Philby or his network.

Angleton was nothing if not thorough. Obsessively so. Finally, on Rick's sixth day in the Archives, Angleton appeared to finish the subject of Operation Phoenix—at least temporarily—and switched his attention to Europe. In particular, he focused on the Czech Revolution of 1968 and its brutal suppression by the Warsaw Pact Forces: primarily the military of the Soviet Union led by Premier Leonid Brezhnev. Every now and then a familiar name would turn up in Angleton's narrative: "Reitenhauser"; and his coveted mole inside the Soviet Union, Code-Name, "Carlton"; Douglas Booker; CIA higher-ups William E. Colby and Richard Helms; former OSS Director William (Wild Bill) Donovan; Allen Dulles and CIA Director John McCone. There were frequent references to Angleton's British Secret Service Counterpart, Nicholas Elliott, for whom he expressed admiration and respect. Rick wondered if Elliott was le Carré's model for his famous character, George Smiley.

By 4:00 p.m. on day 6, Rick felt an overwhelming urge to dose off. He had made no break-through in days and was losing confidence that he would again. But then out of nowhere and with no lead up to it, Angleton wrote the following sentences: "The suppression by the U.S.S.R. of the Czech Revolution was aided by Kim Philby, then a higher-up in the N.K.V.D., the Soviet Intelligence Agency. Philby had, since his defection in '63, been painstakingly building a network of well-placed spies in Prague. He also had developed a counterpart network in the United States, who were busy feeding false information to the CIA and State Department as to the identity of a number of officials in the Czech government who supported the Czech Revolution leader, Alexander Dubcek. Those identified were reported to have been targeted by the NKVD for either arrest or liquidation. The result was that the U.S. warned the wrong people and the Soviets' coup was culminated when the NKVD arrested or shot many entirely different persons."

Then came the breakthrough Rick had been hoping for:

"Philby's network in the U.S. is believed to be composed of the following persons, working under the rubric of a cover organization known as Harp Affiliates, Inc."

The entry was made on January 9, 1970 and directly below it appeared a chart. Rick's most dreaded fears were confirmed when he read it:

```
                HARP AFFILIATES, INC.
                  Organization Chart

President: Foster Wright, alias Quentin Quarles, alias
                        "Q"
     First Vice President:        Second Vice President:
     Ohio Gov. Mark Scherzer      Former CIA Officer Paul
                                  Spence


                     Secretary,
                 Identity unknown


                     Treasurer,
                 Identity unknown

Board of Directors:

Foster Wright
Mark Scherzer
Paul Spence
```

Though certainly depressed that his father-in-law might be a dangerous criminal, Rick's excitement still almost spilled over into a hasty decision to email each of his top investigators and assign them to working up full profiles on Q, Scherzer and Spence. But once he suppressed his excitement enough to think straight, he thought better of it. He needed to complete his search of Angleton's Journals to determine whether there were additions or deletions to the list of three men implicated thus far.

It was now 5:00 p.m. but he felt driven to finish. After buying his dinner from the snack machine (four packages of peanut butter crackers and a diet coke) he let the combination of caffeine and adrenalin take over. He tore through the 1970 and 1971 journals in less than an hour. No more organizational charts or mentions of Harp Affiliates. He ate as he read and by 9:30 p.m. had finished 1972 through 1974. Lots of fascinating new revelations about Watergate, but nothing on Philby or his successors. Those journals did confirm what he always believed that the CIA had played no part in Watergate. It was strictly a rogue operation created by the Nixon Administration with help from former CIA operative, E. Howard Hunt, its architect.

The journal for 1975 proved to be the most philosophical. It was rich in the techniques and theories Angleton had adopted over a lifetime of planning or unraveling clandestine operations.

Several sections described, and provided examples of what Angleton called "The Trust" which was the science of feeding just enough genuine intelligence to an enemy service so that it came to trust you or your agent and conclude that it had successfully doubled the resource in question, when in fact the resource remained wholly loyal to the originator of the trust. Philby was a genius as to the workings of "The Trust," having fooled every member nation of NATO into believing in his undivided loyalty.

Angleton, a mole hunter extraordinaire, was equally adept at seeing through a "Trust" and exposing it. But he admitted to himself that he had a blind spot (as had Elliott) when it came to Philby.

Somewhat more intellectually challenging was the method Angleton called "The Perimeter." He described taking a piece of construction paper and printing in the center of the page a simple assumption he had made. Then he drew around the stated assumption a large circle. Along the perimeter of the circle he would write the things which were likely true if he accepted the central assumption as fact. There was nothing particularly clever about the technique. Its main function appeared to be to impose a discipline on one's mind when trying to think through a cypher. In parenthesis next to Angleton's description of the technique there was written, "(See J.J.A. '76 page 97)."

Rick wasted no time turning to page 97 of the 1976 journal. Page 97 contained the last entry in the '76 journal and therefore, the last entry period, made by Angleton in the series of notebooks. Again, Angleton had drawn an organizational chart:

```
HARP AFFILIATES, INC.
Organization Chart

President: Foster Wright, alias Quentin Quarles, alias
                          "Q"
   First Vice President:        Second Vice President:
   Ohio Gov. Mark Scherzer      Former CIA Officer Paul
                                Spence


             Secretary,
     Henry Hajib, FBI Senior Agent


             Treasurer,
         Identity unknown

Board of Directors:

Foster Wright
Mark Scherzer
Paul Spence
```

Denial again clutched Rick's psyche. A force so powerful that he found himself chuckling at the absurdity of the notion that a respected senior agent of the FBI could be a career-long member of an espionage conspiracy directed against the United States of America. But once again he recognized his naïveté. History was full of unlikely traitors: Judas Iscariot, Benedict Arnold, Alger Hiss, Robert Hansson, Aldrich Ames, and Kim Philby to name a few. If Arnold—the colonists' most successful general in the Revolutionary War—could betray his country, then why couldn't an apparently honorable agent of the FBI?

Rick quickly placed the journals back on the shelves. Even before he walked out the door of the Archives, his mind was formulating a plan of action, at the same time he was removing his cell phone from his jacket pocket. He would wait until he was completely clear of the complex before pressing the speed dial for Fasbender's phone. Fasbender picked up after the first ring.

"Mort, call everyone stat. Meeting my office 0800 tomorrow."

"It must be important for you to revert to military time."

"I didn't realize I did, but it is."

Rick walked into his office at 0759 hours. Everyone else was already there—a good sign. And the coffee maker was percolating. Rick silently congratulated himself for having Maintenance and Supply bring in a 15-foot conference table and extend it to form a T with the back of his desk. Seated at the table and exuding an air of heady anticipation were his four in-house field investigators, seated in no particular order around the table, plus Fasbender, Torres and Black.

Rick placed a poster covered by brown wrapping paper on a stand behind his desk and flush with the back wall. He tore the paper away and got to work without bothering with any preamble.

Beneath the paper was a four by four poster recreating the diagram he found in Angleton's '76 journal.

Allowing his team to first examine it for about a minute, he then spoke for the first time:

"What you see before you is an innocent-looking organizational chart, probably similar to many you've seen before. We have good reason to believe, however, that the four men whose names appear on the chart are the furthest thing from innocent. Each of them likely poses a dangerous threat to the U.S. and its allies. Memorize their names and titles. You will get to hear their names and learn their daily routines over the next several weeks, better than your own."

"There are four names on the chart and eight of us." Rick paused for a couple of seconds to glance at Fasbender in order to gauge his reaction. As he guessed, shock registered in Fasbender's eyes, but he wore no other facial expressions. Fasbender knew Paul Spence and his relationship to Rick.

"We'll divide into four squads: A-Squad, Torres and MacDougal will cover Scherzer; B-Squad, Black and Mineo on Hajib; C-Squad, Fasbender and Hirsch take Foster Wright and D-Squad Dubinsky and I will take Spence."

Elayne Hirsch was a counterintelligence officer on loan from the Navy. The three other investigators were career CIA.

"Research your subjects thoroughly. If one of them was suspended from college for a fraternity prank, I want to know about it. Just as much as I want to know who they socialize with, what they do in their spare time; what clubs they belong to; whether they've ever been arrested; what honors they've received. If they're married, how many times, and to whom. What are their tastes in food, drink, books, music, movies, sports and politics? Did they serve in the military and if so, what's in their 201 files? What of their family background?"

"We have carte blanche. You'll each be issued credentials that will get you into the darkest corners and deepest rabbit holes of the government."

"I will give you each a secure email address. You are to report to me in detail every evening before 2200 hours on what you learned that day. And you only have three weeks so you better get going. I want to assemble the most comprehensive dossiers ever."

"We'll meet every Sunday night right here at 1900 hours, sharp. The only excuse for not attending will be a work assignment elsewhere. There will be no notices or reminders."

"Mort will give you a secure phone number. Use it only for the most dire emergencies. Good luck!"

"Right now you'll all meet with Mort in the East Conference Room to discuss your mission in more detail. I'll see you back here in one week. Dubinsky, report back to me when you're through." The group of seven filed out silently without asking any questions. With the exception of Torres they were all pros, and she was the quickest study he had ever met.

He was comfortable with his team and could now get to the

business of working Angleton's perimeter. Rick took a fresh piece of blank 8 ½ x 14 paper out of his printer and laid it on his desk. He placed it sideways and drew a circle reaching close to the edges of the paper.

At the center of the circle he printed: "1. SPENCE: HOSTILE." His silent question was, "If that assumption is true, what else is likely to be true?"

He worked the possibilities. In the bar at his and Clarissa's wedding celebration, Spence had revealed inside information on Rick's new role in the U.N. investigation. This was top secret information that to the best of his knowledge, only Doug Booker, the President and his inner circle knew about.

Rick mulled it over for several minutes before making his first entry on the perimeter: "Spence likely penetrated White House."

Chapter Eleven

ANGLETON'S CIRCLE

Mort Fasbender and Ensign Elayne Hirsch, nicknamed Ellie, had just left Langley where they had divided the hundred pages of Q's personnel file into two roughly equal segments, one for each of them. Hirsch studied pages 1 through 47; Fasbender, 48 through 100. It was like rummaging through a trunk full of costume jewelry in search of the Hope Diamond. They didn't find any diamonds but it wasn't all junk either. Their search did yield a few gems.

As they sped south on the interstate in a Nissan Maxima just checked out of the motor pool, Ellie, who habitually drove fast, spoke even faster—both with enthusiasm. "What's really interesting is that Wright seems not to have even existed before 1961, when he showed up as CIA Station Chief in Munich. Then for an encore, he disappears off the face of the map in 1976 as if abducted by aliens. And his file says nothing about what happened to him. Had he been murdered? Died of natural causes? Defected? Ran? What do you think, Mort?"

"My guess is none of the above. It's more likely he went deep underground. Maybe he still is. The only residential address was the one in Savannah, so that's where we're headed."

In addition to the discovered residential address, two other valuable pieces of information were contained in the personnel file. The first was that from 1969 through 1974, Q sent a series of handwritten letters to his Deputy Chief of Munich Station, "Spencer Pauley." The second was that in the last letter dated November 9, 1974, Q asked Pauley if he had submitted Q's application for a visa to the Soviet Union so he could attend the Trade and Currency Conference. It appeared from the context that Harp Affiliates was an operational cover organization at least in 1974 and probably for many years before and after.

These disclosures were reported to Rick via email that evening at 2145 hours, right after he had opened one from Torres reporting that Scherzer and Pauley had flown together via Lufthansa to Moscow on January 17, 1975. Rick made three new entries in the Angleton Circle with corresponding notes at the perimeter. On January 15, 1975, Scherzer had just been sworn in as a first-term congressman from Ohio and was immediately appointed to the House International Commerce Committee.

Ellie Hirsch was a pert and pretty late twenty-something with a high energy motor and a supple mind. She came highly recommended by Admiral Otis Branford, Chief of Naval Intelligence. Though she had started her career as an intelligence analyst, the Navy soon learned that her real talents lay in the area of counterintelligence. They made her a C.I. investigator at the age of 23 and she had left a whirlwind in her path ever since.

At 1130 hours Fasbender used his cell phone to make reservations for rooms at a Best Western in Wilmington, North Carolina. He and Hirsch checked in about midnight and ordered wakeup calls for each room for 6:00 a.m. They knew that time was of the essence but had been up since 5:00 a.m. and needed to grab some sleep. The next day they would drive straight through to Savannah.

At 0930 hours Mort and Ellie, with Mort behind the wheel this time, entered the leafy Savannah Historic District. The lush central-city park, rich with 100-year-old trees and war monuments, even older, clothed the area with a serene aura.

The mapped route on the GPS screen in front of Ellie made her job as navigator easy. She directed Mort to turn left onto a scenic cobblestone street bordered on each side by ivy-covered town houses. Two more turns and they were on Bay Street headed south toward the Savannah watershed and the city's port on the Savannah River. The address they had for Q was 18 Hilltop Path. A right turn at the lower port and short drive past half a dozen high-end looking seafood houses led them to a narrow street onto which they made a right turn and began a slow ascension up a narrow and winding two-way lane. At the top of the long climb was a ramshackle Victorian mansion—going to seed—lawn overgrown by weeds; broken shutters; peeling paint; shingles scattered on the ground; an impassable 50-foot driveway; cracked windows and a water damaged front door.

They parked on the street after eyeing an estate sign tilted at a 45-degree angle, announcing that the address of the rambling monstrosity was 18 Hilltop Path.

After stepping over felled trees and plodding through the growth, they finally stood on a crumbling front stoop. There was no door bell but staring at them was an iron door knocker fashioned into the face of the designer's concept of a Silas Marner or Nicholas Nickleby.

Fasbender gave it three quick raps and then waited. Each of them patted their service revolvers from which they gathered reassurance; then a second series of raps but still no answer. Hirsch was confident that with a building of this size they would find a way in without having to break anything. But as she turned to make a search they heard a creaking noise reminiscent of a Bella Lugosi movie. Fasbender and Hirsch situated themselves at either side of the door as it slowly creaked open.

Not knowing what to expect they were not surprised when standing in front of them was a diminutive man, in his late 70s or early 80s, dressed in a brown suit, white dress shirt and paisley tie. A glint of fear shone in his eyes. He looked up at Mort and Ellie but did not speak.

"Federal Agents," said Mort, as they flashed their badges. Still no response from their greeter.

"Is there anyone else in the house besides you?"

A slow nod of his head from side to side.

"We would like to come in and speak with you."

The elderly man granted his permission by simply moving out of the center of the doorway. Mort and Ellie scanned the hallway before entering, with weapons drawn; but had to settle for taking only limited precautions. There was no way they could clear what they guesstimated to be over fifty rooms.

Their greeter looked at their credentials with mild curiosity, but without comment.

Fasbender did the talking.

"Please tell us your name, sir."

"Edmund De Télliér."

"Do you live here?"

A nod in the negative.

"Do you know who does?"

"No one does."

"Do you mind telling us what you are doing here?"

"Yes."

"You do mind?"

"Yes."

"Why would that be?"

"You're not the police."

"That's true, sir, but we are conducting an investigation vital to national security and we need your help."

"I'm the caretaker. Live about a quarter mile up the road."

"I see. Who is your employer?"

"I don't know if I have to answer that question."

"Technically, you don't now but eventually you will. Let me try it another way. Is your employer named Foster Wright?"

"No."

"Quentin Quarles?"

"He's one of them. There are two."

"Is your other employer Mark Scherzer?"

"No. Never heard of him."

"Malcolm Flaherty?"

"No. That's a trick question; he's the head of the FBI. The other one is Mr. Pauley."

"Do you know his first name?"

"Yes, Spencer; but Mr. Quarles and Mr. Pauley are not my real employers. They just work for the owner."

"Which is whom?"

"A corporation but I can't remember its name right now. Here's its card."

De Télliér produced a business card from a suit coat pocket. Embossed with gold lettering on the front was "Harp Affiliates, Inc." Fasbender stuck it in his own pocket.

"When was the last time you saw Quentin Quarles?"

"I've never seen Mr. Quarles or Mr. Pauley. Only spoke to them on the phone. They send a woman to meet with me. I know her only as Miss Webb."

"Can you describe her?"

"She's about average height, blond hair, in her late thirties or early forties. Pretty. I think she's somehow related to Mr. Quarles or Mr. Pauley.

"Why do you think that?"

"I don't know. I've had this job for twelve years. It was just something somebody said. I don't remember who said it, or when. My memory's not what it used to be."

Neither Mort nor Ellie detected any evasiveness in the man's manner. Ellie decided to give it another shot. Using her most gentle and disarming demeanor she softly asked, "Mr. De Télliér, would you try to remember? It's very important. I happen to know, as a woman, that if there are two men you never see and one woman you see often, the woman is more likely to lower her guard and speak of a personal matter."

De Télliér pondered this. It seemed to have registered some place after about thirty seconds of apparently searching his memory. He responded:

"I think it was about seven or eight years ago. I'm not sure, but I remember Miss Webb was pleased with the work done by the contractor I used to repair the roof...the roof of the gables...she was in a good mood...the holiday season and all...she said something about how pleased Mr. Quarles and Mr. Pauley would be when she told them about it at the family's Christmas Dinner. Sorry, I can't... That's all I can remember."

"Sir, have you ever seen anyone here besides Miss Webb?" De Télliér lapsed into his deep southern drawl. "Oh my, yes! Mostly men, but some women too, come in and out all the time. Some leave the same day; others have stayed as long as a few weeks. I don't know who they are and I usually get only about an hour's notice; but our housekeeping agency doesn't mind the short notice at all. They've gotten plenty of business from my employer over the last dozen years or so. I never know when I'm going to get a call so I try to get over there at least once a day."

That night, Rick Tallifierro made the following entry inside his Angleton circle:

"Q, P.S. and related woman manage safe houses owned by Harp."

He drew an arrow to the perimeter and printed:

```
"Q apparently lives. He's likely
Spence's father or uncle and Cl's
grandfather or great uncle."
```

Next, Rick emailed Fasbender and Hirsch:

> "Keep house under surveillance and take any visitors into custody."

His email to Dubinsky was even more succinct:

> "Put Spence under 24-hour surveillance and report to me only."

He turned off all the lights in his office, drank a shot of brandy and began to plan his inevitable confrontation with Clarissa.

Chapter Twelve

TORRES AND MAC DOUGAL

Several shots hit MacDougal. A spray of bullets had been fired at MacDougal and Torres while on the steps of the Capitol Building. Only one shot hit Torres, in her right calf. Having recently completed her CIA training course, she recognized the sound as that of an AR-15 assault rifle. MacDougal was hit in the neck, chest, stomach and groin. It was bad. Torres did not seek cover. She removed a bandana from her jacket pocket and quickly tied it around her wound.

She then tried to minister to MacDougal, tying his light windbreaker tightly around the chest wound while she put pressure on his stomach wound with her left hand. With her right hand she pulled her cellphone out of its case and pushed the speed dial for the emergency number. Rick answered without delay. "Agent down on Capitol steps, send paramedics stat!"

"Copy that. Find cover!"

Torres found a handkerchief in MacDougal's jacket pocket and tied it around the neck wound, which was bleeding profusely. The bullet probably hit an artery. She had nothing else to apply to the groin wound so she used her own jacket with "2014 U.S. Women's Golf Open" printed in bright yellow on the back; and it seemed to stanch the flow of blood from that wound. But after some initial agonized moans from the pain, MacDougal lapsed into unconsciousness. His breathing was shallow and pulse weak. He was in shock and bleeding out.

Torres was crying softly with her left hand still on his stomach wound when the ambulance arrived eleven minutes after the shooting.

Two paramedics gently pulled her away and placed her on a stretcher while two others tried to administer CPR to MacDougal. It was too late; Agent MacDougal had expired. Torres was not an experienced law enforcement officer and had to fight against going into hysterics. By a sheer act of will she managed to substitute prayer for hysteria. She was still praying when they wheeled her into the Emergency Room of Walter Reed Hospital.

Rick's office had the look and feel of a crisis center. Tom Tallifierro manned the phones. A long-time CIA operations clerk, Gloria Duncan, handled reception and screened calls for him.

Rick ordered Dubinsky to stand down from his assignment until further notice. No point risking the life of another operative until they had a better handle on what was going on. Fasbender and Hirsch were given no new orders other than to get their assault weapons out of the trunk and reduce their own visibility.

A CIA ambulance using the cover name of a private service arrived at the Capitol scene and took MacDougal's body away.

Rick could not allow himself to mourn MacDougal. He needed every bit of concentration he could muster. The reassuring presence of his father helped.

There would be no public funeral for MacDougal, just a private ceremony at Arlington National Cemetery—attended by only his immediate family, an Agency Chaplain and a few CIA officials. His death, like much of his life, would be shrouded in anonymity. At some undetermined time in the future there'd be a private in memoriam service at Langley and his name would be posted on a wall of honor.

*   *   *

Stanislaw (Stan) Dubinsky took the news like the pro he was, even though his shock and grief were profound. Matt MacDougal was his best friend; their wives were best friends and their children were growing up together. He fought off the almost irresistible tug to rush to the side of MacDougal's family. But he was a soldier and a soldier did not flee the battlefield. Rick had pulled him off his tail of Spence but had redirected him to the headquarters of the Secret Service where he would try to find out if Spence was on the list of those who had access to the White House; and if so, who put him on it.

*   *   *

Fasbender and Hirsch, having the element of surprise and superior firepower on their side, had no problem taking into custody two armed callers at the mansion. Both were male Caucasians in their mid-to-late thirties. One of them had ten thousand dollars in cash in his pocket. Fasbender called for backup, who appeared on the scene in about twenty minutes and transported the two detainees to a CIA detention facility in the hills surrounding McLean, Virginia.

*   *   *

Rick got a call from his contact at the N.S.A., Ed Chalmers, who gave him the bad news that the uptick in phone traffic among hundreds of terrorist suspects and the dramatic increase in phone, email and text intercepts pointed to a mounting threat of a new terrorist attack in the United States.

*   *   *

Walter Black and Joe Mineo worked on the mainframe computer at FBI Headquarters, their alleged job being to install an updated hard-drive with ten times the memory capacity. Their real mission was to download all emails to and from Agent Henry Hajib over the past year, to their own laptops. Their cover was as FBI career computer geeks who roved from office to office. The Op Shop had outdone itself in altering their facial characteristics and supplying them with back-stopped and impeccable credentials. Hajib's electronic mail turned out to be a treasure trove. Included in his sent and received mail were messages to and from top Al Qaeda and ISIS leaders in Yemen, Pakistan, Libya, Iraq and Syria. They were in deep cover, from which they would not emerge until the completion of their assignment.

*   *   *

Torres would be lost to Rick for at least two weeks. He was now down one team and had to do something, and fast. It was probably too late to integrate new people into the mission. They didn't have enough time to be adequately briefed and he didn't have the time to brief them. But he did have Tom Tallifierro.

"Dad, do you think you can run this place for a while? I need to go operational. I can't leave Dubinsky out there by himself."

"No sweat. It will be a throw-back to my Army Intelligence Days. I was always the headquarters guy pulling the strings of our field agents. Ben had all the fun and glamour. He was the best field operative I ever knew. Our superstar. The Babe Ruth of spooks. But, just be careful out there."

"I will; but as long as you mentioned Ben Berger, any chance you can seduce him back into the game. We could really use him. He's special."

"Well, we haven't had much contact in recent years. But...*maybe*."

"Tell him his country needs him, and we need him too. But don't email him. Call him."

"When do you want him to start?"

"As soon as he hangs up the phone."

"He's 72 years old but I'm told by mutual friends that he's healthy as a horse and as strong as a bull. He ran in both the New York and Boston Marathons last year."

"Heh, I'm no ageist anyway. Let's try to sign him up a.s.a.p."

"I know you're no ageist, otherwise I wouldn't be here."

Tom smiled and picked up the phone.

*   *   *

"Ben, it's Tom."

"Ah, to what do I owe the pleasure?"

"First I want to apologize for the little jurisdictional spat we had on Project Lodestone. I was out of line and unfair to you; and also unfair to the Bureau."

"Heh—it was seven years ago and I got over it a long time ago. Besides I wasn't exactly an innocent bystander. We both were at fault."

"Yeah, a little bit too much testosterone on both sides. But still, I'm really relieved there's no hard feelings."

"None. So what can I do for you, old buddy?"

"I'll save the details until we get together, but the long and the short of it is, Rick needs you."

"Fine, but on one condition. My partner has to join us and be part of it."

Taken aback for a second, Tom quickly gathered himself. "Who's your partner?"

"I won't tell you that over the phone. He'll be with me when we get together. But I will say that he has the necessary background and credentials."

Tom knew instantly who Ben had in mind. "How about breakfast tomorrow at 0800, Georgetown Motor Inn?"

"Unlike the old days, I promise not to be late."

* * *

It was FBI Agent Hajib's email of the previous day to Kyle Collins, intercepted by Black and Mineo, which caused Rick to pull Fasbender and Hirsch from the Savannah mansion and send them racing north on U.S. 1 towards Charleston. The email was only one sentence—17 words—but its portent was immeasurable:

> "She wants Mark, Q, Pauley and me at the Citadel for a meet on 3/23 at 0900."

One could fairly deduce that "Mark" was Mark Scherzer. "She" was a bit more mysterious.

As Fasbender chatted with Rick via car phone, Clarissa boarded a Delta Airlines flight at LaGuardia Airport, destination St. Augustine, stopping at Baltimore, Virginia Beach, Wilmington, N.C., Charleston, Savannah and Jacksonville.

Fasbender and Hirsch both noted the prominent road sign, "Cape Fear 20 miles." Rick was then briefing them on Torres' condition, his conversation with MacDougal's widow and the heads-up from N.S.A.

The juxtaposition of Rick's report with the "Cape Fear" sign felt ominous.

* * *

As it turned out, a certain phone call Rick received a couple of days later caused him to pull Fasbender and Hirsch from Charleston. ISIS was stretching the capacity of Rick's small group to fulfill its mission. NSA had reported quickly burgeoning text, email and phone communications from ISIS' headquarters in Raqqa. One particular email was so alarming that Rick pointed Mort and Ellie in a northerly direction once again.

Chapter Thirteen

TWO WOMEN

It had been ten years since Clarissa had seen her sister. Had the present occasion not arisen, it might have been another decade or longer before they met again. Although there was only two years' age difference between them, they were not close growing up.

In most ways, they were total opposites. Deidre Wilson was then an extroverted party girl and school politician with a nonstop social life. Clarissa was the object of admiration by many fellow students, but was essentially a reserved and quiet book worm with a flair for dramatic arts. She spent most of her free time in the village library. It was no accident that Clarissa was now a top litigator while Deidre was a part-time model known mainly as a party planner and hostess for hire.

Both, however, considered their upcoming reunion to be important and approached it without reservation. Their relationship had been less a victim of friction than of benign neglect. Charleston was chosen as the site because of the activity of mutual concern planned for the city. That their father, Paul Spence, was the catalyst for bringing them together on this occasion was typical of the family dynamics which had been in place since their preteen years.

Clarissa had no difficulty recognizing Deidre at the baggage carousel. Over the years she had seen her picture in the gossip columns and in various magazines. Deidre was still pretty but the soft brown eyes that had won the heart of many a callow teenage boy had hardened and now displayed a cynical worldliness.

As Deidre approached—dressed in stylish black pants and a silk patterned blouse, accessorized by an expensive looking Armani handbag—Clarissa felt a twinge of regret tempered by an unexpected sense of joy. She loved her older sister but unfortunately that emotion did not carry with it even the smallest degree of respect.

Deidre felt quite the opposite. Her respect and admiration for Clarissa was unbridled, but love was not part of the package; at least that was what she thought. Her ability to admire was capacious— especially when it came to Clarissa—but she believed she had lost the capacity for love, if indeed she ever had it. A platoon of ex-husbands and former lovers would willingly offer testimony to that fact. One of those now-former lovers was Prescott Burns, the Director of the CIA.

The sisters did not embrace or even exchange kisses. They both smiled broadly and engaged in meaningless small talk about the plane trip, traffic to the airport, the warm weather, each other's outfits and current hair styles.

Not until they were comfortably seated in the voice-proof rear compartment of Deidre's chauffeured limousine, and each sipped a dry martini, did they venture beyond the banal and the trivial.

"Have you seen Dad yet?"

"Yes, far more often than I would have liked since I arrived the day before yesterday."

Clarissa responded only with a rueful smile.

A silence engulfed them for several minutes, a type of dead air which would have been fatal to a radio talk-show host. It was as if each had exhausted her script.

Deidre was the first to break the silence.

"You know Clarissa; Burns is fully aware that Rick is conducting a parallel investigation."

"I assumed as much but also assumed that he was too smart to reveal his knowledge to the higher-ups."

"Yes, his only tangible reaction has been to reduce Crowe's investigation to an empty shell. Crowe is totally pissed but lacks the cojönes to do anything about it."

"What does Dad think about all this?"

"Who knows? You know Dad; he only lets you in on what he wants you to know. Incidentally, I haven't told him that I brought you into town. He'll be out at the Citadel for the next few days, so we'll have time to decide whether or not to break the news. What about Rick?"

"Rick spends virtually all his time in the office these days, so he's oblivious to my comings and goings. I simply told him I was going to visit mother for a few days. He just grunted his approval. He knows how lonely she's been since the divorce."

The sisters once again lapsed into a comfortable silence, secure in their belief that their meeting was unknown to anyone but themselves. But as they crossed the bridge over the Cooper River and headed south towards Charleston Harbor, they had company. The nondescript beige Hyundai stayed just close enough behind them to keep them in view, but not close enough to be detected. Behind the wheel of the Hyundai was Chris Berger. Next to him in the passenger seat was his father, Ben.

*　　*　　*

Later, on the broad patio of the graceful "Charleston South Hotel," with a magnificent view of the Harbor, Ben and Chris worked out their itinerary. Ben's FBI background would give him the access he needed to wander about the Citadel for the next couple of days while Chris kept an eye on the Spence sisters.

As a former FBI station chief in Charleston, Ben would call in all his old chits to see if he could learn the time and location of the four-way meeting. He knew already that Scherzer would have to attend incognito given his high degree of face recognition.

*   *   *

"You and I have to meet ASAP!"

"Calm down Stan, said Rick, who had never before heard Stanislaw Dubinsky so agitated."

"Right...when you hear what I have to say you won't be so calm either."

"Copy that. I'll see you in fifteen minutes at the Pulaski Grill. Do whatever you have to do to get us our usual rear table next to the kitchen doors."

Fourteen minutes later, Dubinsky sat with his back to the wall at the pre-selected rear table. In his preoccupation with what he had learned, he barely noticed the nonstop swinging of the doors to the kitchen. And though parsimonious (many preferred "cheap"), he was untroubled by the $100.00 dollar bill it had cost him to have the table's occupants relocated. Clandestine conferences were frequently held at the Pulaski and the rear tables were in demand.

Dubinsky was still shaken by MacDougal's murder and exchanged only a quick handshake with Rick as he sat down opposite him.

Rick was painfully aware of the necessity among intelligence professionals to maintain an even strain as part of one's façade. Yet he also tried never to ignore the human factor. Now he believed that something needed to be said to Dubinsky.

"I'm very sorry for your loss, Stan. I know how close you and Mac were."

"Well, we soldier on. There will be time to grieve after these bastards are either doing life without parole in a federal pen or pushing up daisies." Dubinsky's facial expression combined sadness, anger and resolve in equal measure.

"So what's your news Stan?"

"The betrayal runs wide and deep. My sources at the Secret Service, who by the way are first rate, have been just waiting for an operation like ours to come along. They have already filed a report with the Deputy Director of the FBI, Clyde Underwood, who supposedly is working sub-rosa to gather enough evidence on Hajib and Scherzer to bring to the Attorney General. When it all hits the fan, it may make Watergate look like pilfering the White House pantry."

"In the meantime, my sources tell me that Kyle Collins is the unofficial liaison between the O.D.N.I. and the National Security Council. Because of Spence's CIA background and clout in both political parties, Collins has cajoled and maneuvered to position him as a top intelligence advisor to the Council. Sort of their secret ombudsman for purposes of keeping an eye on the CIA. Spence's access to the Council and oversight of the CIA is like putting the fox in charge of the hen house; and his access to the White House is said to run deep. The National Security Advisor reports only to the President and his Chief of Staff. The current National Security Advisor, Myron Polk, happens to work closely with the Chief of Staff, giving Spence a pipeline to the Oval Office. And the whole set-up is closely monitored by Collins."

"But, Underwood won't go to the AG until he has undisputable evidence. You can't really blame him."

"No," said Rick, "we are faced with the same problem. Everything we have so far as evidence of a criminal conspiracy is circumstantial. I hope when the big pow-wow now going on at the Citadel is over, we'll have a lot more. Does the President know about Spence?"

"My sources think not. Hajib, a senior FBI agent, and Collins are adept at running a cover-up."

"Stan, with the loss of MacDougal and temporary sidelining of Torres, I've had to beef-up our troops. One of my father's colleagues, Ben Berger, and his son, Chris, are already operational."

"How is Torres doing?"

"Not bad but the shot tore through a lot of sinew and muscle in her calf and she's hobbled right now. I think her main worry is that she'll miss the excitement when we finally move in on the bad guys."

"When do you think that'll be?"

"Hard to say because the landscape changes daily and sometimes hourly. But I can't help but think that right now Charleston is the key."

*   *   *

Clarissa sipped from a cup of Seattle's Finest French Roast coffee while she tried to organize the jumble of thoughts in her mind. She did not want her first full day in Charleston to go for naught. Meanwhile Deidre noisily stumbled around the bathroom of their luxurious hotel suite, readying herself for the day's events. When she emerged she wore a stylish business suit and high heels, but betrayed an uncommon nervousness. Her reply to Clarissa's question as to where she was headed was a curt, "nowhere important." When Clarissa asked if she wanted company, her response was even more unpleasant. "No, but if you must have something to do, you can stop at housekeeping and pick up my laundry."

Clarissa bristled but decided not to address Deidre's blatant rudeness, attributing it partly to her nervous state. But the good feelings between them of the previous afternoon and evening were clearly over.

Grabbing her pocketbook and a soft leather briefcase, Deidre bolted out the door, mumbling that she would call if she had time. Add one more troubling thought to the mish-mash already infesting Clarissa's psyche.

But, Clarissa wasn't a top trial lawyer for no reason. Her inner toughness kept her from being stymied for long. Until she decided on her next step, she figured that she might as well pick up Deidre's laundry. It would give her a chance to roam around the hotel a bit and get the lay of the land. After making a quick inspection of the main ballroom, restaurant, swimming pool, rec room, salon and gift shop, she checked the hotel directory and saw that "Housekeeping/Laundry" was in the basement. From the lobby she entered an elevator and pressed "B." The enormous footprint of the Charleston South gave Clarissa a lengthy walk through the basement corridors before she finally found the room marked "Housekeeping/Laundry." She entered and was greeted by a young and attractive African-American woman behind the counter.

"Can I help you, madam?"

"Yes," said Clarissa, as she placed down the laundry ticket Deidre had carelessly thrown on their kitchen table.

The counter lady noted the ticket number and smiled with relief. "I was hoping you would come to pick up your laundry, sooner rather than later."

"Oh, why is that?"

"Because this note fell out of your raincoat pocket when we separated your things. Here it is. This is a load off my mind. All we had was the ticket stub and didn't know how to contact you."

Clarissa's curiosity was clearly piqued. The note was a folded piece of 5 by 7 stationery with a scented aroma. She thanked the young woman and signed for the laundry, consisting of three casual outfits, two evening dresses and a raincoat. She stuffed the unread note in her pocketbook and took her leave. Before doing so, however, she removed two crisp twenty dollar bills from her purse, thanked the woman for her concern and placed the twenties on the counter.

Clarissa was consumed by curiosity as to what was in the note but did not want to take it to their room to read, for the chance that Deidre might come back unexpectedly and catch her reading it. Instead, after dropping off the laundry in their room, she left the hotel and walked south a few blocks to the Battery. She found a bench in a small park with a view of Fort Sumter in the distant reaches of the harbor, removed the note from her pocketbook and began reading:

> "The just are innocent of violence
> and carnage. And Quest's objectives
> are right and just. The terror
> occasionally caused by those
> benefitting from our activities is
> incidental and collateral. We remain
> blameless because violence is not
> part of our credo. Quest's sublime
> goal of dismantling and reducing to
> rubble the intelligence capacity of
> the evil behemoth, the United States
> of America, is exalted in all ways.
> We enjoy permanent exoneration for
> the horrors inflicted by those who
> may have been enabled or facilitated
> by our excellent work. These are the
> core beliefs of our founder and
> inspiration, The Great Philby."

*   *   *

Clarissa reread the note three times before folding it and placing it in the right back pocket of her jeans. She sat and stared at the handsome cabs and open-sided tourist busses passing through her line of sight. After roughly fifteen minutes of staring straight ahead in a trance-like stupor, she slowly rose to her feet; removed her cell phone from her bag and dialed a familiar number.

*   *   *

None of the four corporate officers of Harp Associates, Inc. hailed from South of the Mason-Dixon line and were, therefore, caught off guard when informed at the entrance gate that all official business at the Citadel was suspended for three hours while the annual ceremonies celebrating Robert E. Lee Day were in progress at the Parade Grounds. They knew, however, that they must attend the ceremonies lest they insult their host, the commandant of the academy.

Their inconvenience worked to Ben Berger's advantage. He had used his still considerable clout at the FBI—especially with Deputy Director Clyde Underwood—to have the FBI's legendary COINTELPRO domestic intelligence group standing by. Upon Berger's phone call to Underwood at 8:00 a.m., a team of COINTELPRO surveillance experts was dispatched to the Citadel, from the FBI's Charleston office, and at the military academy installed a full array of covert listening devices and a hidden video recorder in the small annex to the main building. There, Q and his cohorts would later hold their meeting. Both the audio and visual would be transmitted to the hotel room of the Berger father-son team. And Chris Berger's surveillance revealed that the Harp group's sweep of the annex had already been done early that morning before their own installations began.

*   *   *

The two Bergers sat on straight-backed chairs in their hotel room. With rapt attention they stared at and listened to what had just come on the screen.

Q, Scherzer, Hajib and Spence sat around a table in the middle of a rustic-looking room having the décor of a hunting lodge. Each of them had a yellow legal pad in front of him. Although casually dressed, they appeared tense and serious. Surprisingly, Spence rather than Q presided over the meeting. His tone was businesslike; his manner officious.

"We first need to discuss Tallifierro. He's crowding us everywhere. Even though he's my son-in-law, much to my displeasure, he's got to go."

"Consider it done," said Q.

"OK good; but just make sure nothing happens to my daughter."

"You can depend on it."

"And while you're at it, take care of Booker too. That pain-in-the-ass has interfered with our business for the last time."

"No problem."

"Okay, will you put out the work order?" Scherzer blanched, while Hajib got up and left the room, as if the technicality of not being present when murder plans were formulated would prevent him from being complicit.

"Not I," said Q. "It's for that reason that we employ a useful functionary."

"Mark, ask Hajib to come back in. Tell him Quest does not suffer cowards lightly." Spence combined the menacing words with his best scowl.

Upon Spence's command, Congressman Scherzer rose and left the room. It was a good five minutes before he returned with a chastened FBI senior agent in tow.

As if the interrupted proceedings were simply the result of a temporary power outage, Spence continued seamlessly.

"A second item: Qaeda has its next objective selected and wants us to float a false target with both the Bureau and the Company. Deidre will plant the deception with her boyfriend, Burns, to take care of the CIA; and I'm counting on you Hank, to spread the word with the FBI Counterterrorism boys. Can you handle that?"

"Yes." Hajib was flattered that Spence used his nickname, "Hank."

"Well I hope so because we're getting paid ten million dollars to make sure this goes off without a hitch. Evidently ISIS has kicked in a big chunk of the purse from the money and other valuables it has been stealing for months from the Assyrian Christians and the Kurds. It goes without saying that Al Qaeda and Islamic Stateists are not people one wants to disappoint."

"What are the targets, both phony and real?" asked Scherzer.

"The phony one is the U.S. nuclear storage facility in the Nevada desert. We won't be told the real target until 48 hours before the attack, just enough time if we happen to be there, to get the hell out of town."

"Another thing," queried Scherzer, "who was responsible for the attack on the steps of the Capitol? That was just plain stupid. I, or members of my staff could just as easily have been in the line of fire."

"Oh," said Q with a mischievous grin and a voice dripping pure sarcasm. "You'd have just taken one for the team, Mark. A thing you should be proud to do."

Scherzer was clearly stunned by the remark but wasn't about to get on the wrong side of the treacherous Q. Ben Berger made a mental note of a potential schism, with Hajib and Scherzer on one side and Spence and Q on the other.

Seeking to perhaps take some of the sting out of the remark, Spence offered a palliative. "Legitimate question, Mark. The answer is that we had nothing to do with it. I don't know how whoever did, found out the two targets were Tallifierro's people. Maybe your man, Kyle Collins, had something to do with it, or even my daughter, Deidre. Not likely, but all I'm saying is we can't really trust anyone."

Chris Berger cast a glance his father's way as if to say, "This guy is so ruthless, he would sell out his own daughter." Ben caught his meaning and nodded his assent.

Unlike Spence, Q proceeded to speak favorably of Deidre's "dedication to the cause, and loyalty."

*   *   *

"Let's move on to a more general topic," said Spence. "I would like each of your opinions as to our overall security status, at this juncture. So far our operations have gone off like clockwork. Philby taught us well and we have successfully employed his strategies. We have nearly crippled the CIA and other U.S. intelligence services over the last thirty years, simply by applying the techniques of "The Trust" and the "Double Cross" plus all the rest of the tradecraft the master taught. So total has been the deception that they never even knew we were doing it to them."

"Of course, we were innocent of the attacks on the U.S. embassies in Kenya and Tanzanika; on the USS *Cole*, Khobar Towers, the World Trade Center and the U.N.—but we can be proud that the attacks would never have happened unless we had greatly weakened Western Intelligence's capacity for early detection and warning. Even those dopey brothers up in Boston could not have pulled off the attack on the Marathon had we not so effectively undermined U.S. counterintelligence."

"Of course, they all had it coming to them, but we can't take blame or credit for the actual attacks."

"And don't forget," interjected Hajib, "that we successfully maneuvered to get that empty suit, Porter Crowe, appointed to command U.S. Counterintelligence."

The others present in the room chuckled appreciatively at Hajib's accurate observation. Q was more amused than any of them, which apparently caused him to sit back in his chair and muse philosophically. "Yes boys, my father—your idol—would be proud of what we have accomplished so far."

And Spence chimed in, "Well, the best is still to come." The casual pleasure they seemed to take in acts of inhumanity was chilling and terrifying.

*   *   *

Richmond Tallifierro's reaction to the audio/video download from the Bergers' hotel computer could not be easily described. A wave of conflicting emotions tossed him about. Foremost, he was exultant over the smoking gun-type evidence against the four traitors, that had fallen into his hands. Five traitors if you counted Collins. His excitement was curbed, however, by the fact that apparently at least one and possibly two of the conspirators (Spence and Deidre) were family members of Clarissa. Rick was happy that the evidence was obtained without further injury or loss of life; but his satisfaction was tempered by the two death sentences handed down for Booker and himself. Then there was his concern over Clarissa's possible role in the ongoing treachery. He prayed each night that she was innocent in all this, but he was clearly worried.

One of the major reasons Rick had been given his critical assignment was the assessment by the higher-ups that under stress he would be able to juggle the most complex emotions and contradictory data almost routinely. It was a rare talent. Now he had to use a good portion of his agent's acumen and bravery just to stay alive; and whatever was left over to convince FBI Deputy Director Clyde Underwood and the President that a plan of action against "Harp" or "Quest," whatever they were calling themselves these days, had to be formulated and then executed quickly. He had no way of knowing the timing of the terrorist attack. Maybe they had some time, but perhaps not. Maybe it was imminent. And for God's sake, Booker had to be both warned and protected!

He had no time for the anger which held him in its grasp. But emotions are not voluntary. What angered him the most was the craven lying by the four malefactors to themselves. It was beyond infuriating that they could simultaneously exonerate themselves of the violence in one breath, and then with no sense of shame give themselves credit for being the facilitators of chaos, death and destruction.

Rick tamped down his anger with a dose of reality, speaking silently to himself. "Why should I be surprised? These are double-sided men. Sometimes triple-sided. And they are the apostles of the most devious double-sided man of them all, Harold Adrian Russell Philby." It is their nature to be duplicitous, even when it comes to themselves. Then after a pause and a sigh, he made a silent and solemn pledge to himself. "We shall defeat them at their own game, so help us God!"

*   *   *

Fasbender and Hirsch sped towards Washington, DC. They

would drive straight through and meet Rick and Dubinsky for breakfast in Georgetown at 8:00 a.m. From the tenor of Mort's phone conversation with the "boss" of a half hour earlier, pivotal decisions were to be made. Rick's choice for the meeting was his Georgetown safe-house, overlooking the "Exorcist Steps" on Prospect Street, to some a symbol of doom.

*   *   *

Booker's location was, hopefully, known only to Rick and the two body guards Rick had commandeered to protect him, "24/7." Booker displayed no fear other than that of being excluded from the critical decisions to come. Rick would make sure that did not happen.

*   *   *

Black and Mineo were also summoned by Rick to the 8:00 a.m. meeting. The Berger father-son tandem was kept in Charleston to monitor the Harp conspirators and to remain on call for deployment to wherever they were needed. Ben Berger was a little too old for physical confrontation, but as a field strategist he had no peers.

*   *   *

Torres was pressed back into service earlier than her doctors had advised but only to assist Tom with the computers and phones at headquarters.

Rick's team was now at full strength and poised to execute the plan arrived at in the Oval Office among himself, Deputy Director Underwood, National Security Director Polk and the President of the United States, with participation by Doug Booker on speaker phone.

Chapter Fourteen

BLUEPRINT FOR SURVIVAL

The pivotal White House meeting of the previous day began at 3:00 p.m. The President presided and conducted the questioning:

"Thank you for meeting with us, Mr. Tallifierro. Mr. Polk has briefed me on the current state of things. Have you come with a plan of action?"

"I have Mr. President but first, if you will bear with me, I would like to fill you in on some key information which, because of its personal and sensitive nature, I have not previously divulged to either Deputy Director Underwood or Director Polk."

"Proceed Mr. Tallifierro."

"Thank you Sir. As you may know, my wife, Clarissa, is an accomplished litigation attorney with the Manhattan firm of Thurman, Bixby and Reed. She is also the younger daughter of Paul Spence. What you may not know is that her older sister is Deidre Wilson, a well-known Manhattan and DC social hostess, whose name has been linked romantically with CIA Director Burns. I strongly suspect that Wilson has had an ulterior motive for the Burns connection."

"What is the basis for your suspicion?"

"About two weeks ago, Ms. Wilson called my wife who had not heard from her in ten years, and suggested that the two of them have a reunion of sorts in Charleston, South Carolina. She told Melissa that she missed her and wanted them to reunite. She quickly added, however, that there were also important matters they needed to discuss that were critical to both their family and to the country. Clarissa tried to press her for details but Deidre said she didn't want to discuss them over the phone. When Clarissa asked, "Why Charleston?" Deidre replied that important events involving their father were afoot there at the Citadel. Clarissa had qualms about accepting the invitation but had been worried about her family since their parents got divorced about seven months ago; and was particularly concerned over her father's unusual—often erratic—behavior since the divorce. She also has had for years a strong desire to resolve family differences. Under the circumstances she didn't see how she could reject her sister's overture."

"Should we be worried about your having too many close, personal connections to one of the main targets of the investigation?"

"Very fair question, Mr. President. I don't believe so but hear me out before you decide."

"Go on."

"When Clarissa and Deidre got together in Charleston, things were fine between them for the first afternoon and evening. They shared a suite in the Charleston Harbor Hotel. But by the morning of the second day, Deidre's attitude had completely changed. Rather than explaining to Clarissa the details of the 'important' matters Deidre had referred to over the phone, she treated Clarissa rudely and dismissively—giving only curt answers to Clarissa's questions. She announced she was going out for the day. When Clarissa asked if she could accompany her, Deidre abruptly answered that if Clarissa really needed something to do, she could pick up Deidre's laundry. Without any exchange of pleasantries, Deidre then walked out the door at about 9:00 a.m. and did not return until 5:00 p.m.

Clarissa was already troubled by Deidre's unsolicited comment in the airport limousine the previous day, that Director Burns knew all about our investigation. But as a lawyer, Clarissa has learned not to react until she has the facts, so she decided to take a tour of the hotel and find other things to do in Charleston to keep herself busy. While on her walking tour, she stopped at the laundry in the hotel basement and picked up Deidre's clothes. Thinking she was Deidre, the laundry attendant gave Clarissa a piece of stationery which she explained had fallen out of Deidre's raincoat pocket.

Clarissa did not read the paper until she had left the hotel for a walk down to the Charleston Battery. There she read it, called to tell me about it and emailed a copy to me."

Rick then pulled an 8 ½ by 11 piece of white copy paper from the inside pocket of his suit coat. "I'll read it to you."

When he had finished reading, Rick looked up to view somber expressions on the faces of the others in the room. But their faces expressed more than just gravity. All three men appeared slightly dazed and bewildered, suggestive of questions unasked and answers unknown.

Underwood was the first to speak:

"Was the handwriting familiar?"

"It was printed in all caps," answered Rick, as he passed the piece of paper around.

"Who has the original?" queried Polk.

"My wife, who is now on a flight back to Washington from Charleston."

Underwood again spoke. "Do you think Wilson simply forgot about the note, or planted it so your wife would find it?"

"I don't know but I think it's more likely she wanted Clarissa to find it. The note was out of Deidre's possession for several days while in the laundry and three more days after Clarissa found it. Yet she apparently made no attempt to retrieve it and never once mentioned it to Clarissa. Her request to Clarissa to pick up her laundry seems more than coincidental."

"Yet," said the President, "your video of the 'Citadel meeting' would seem to point to Wilson as a co-conspirator. Did she at any time talk to your wife about the pressing family issues or other issues of national importance?"

"Not a word, and when Clarissa brought it up, Deidre evaded the issue by claiming that during their previous phone conversation she was overwrought by complications of her relationship with Burns, as well as with her father. She claimed to have overreacted in her use of hyperbole. Clarissa pressed, but could not shake her from her explanation. I can't help but wonder if the only reason Deidre asked Clarissa to meet her in Charleston was to make sure the note fell into Clarissa's hands."

"But how does she know for sure that your wife found and read the piece of paper?" asked Polk.

"The Spences—Paul and Deidre—are, I believe, topflight operators. Clarissa on the other hand is a civilian. Without much difficulty Deidre could have had Clarissa under surveillance during the entire critical period; or she might have simply inquired of the laundry as to whether they had found the note. Or the entire interaction between the laundry attendant and Clarissa could have been a set-up, arranged and paid for by Deidre."

"How do you know so much about Wilson's alleged clandestine activities?" asked Underwood bluntly.

"Over my last nine years as a CIA Counterintelligence analyst, Deidre Wilson has always been on the periphery of suspected hostile espionage. But she's been as elusive as quick silver and we've never been able to directly implicate her. Of course, until my guys bugged the Citadel meeting of HARP we had even less on the Spences. Deidre has seemed to be Harp's one public face. She showed up at the National Counterintelligence Association's annual meeting at the Greenbrier under the guise of being no more than Burns' mistress. But, I personally saw her spending alone time with Crowe as well.

Also, the old gentleman overseer who Fasbender and Hirsch interviewed at Harp's safe-house in Savannah, spoke of a woman apparently related to both Spence and Q who was their on-the-scene contact. His physical description of her sounded a lot like Deidre's.

Now we have Q on a disk referring to Deidre as part of the operation and strongly suggesting that he himself is Philby's son. Our records search already pointed to Spence as Q's son. If all that is so, Deidre would be Philby's great-granddaughter and presumably part of a strong gene pool of spies and conspirators."

"Well, couldn't the same thing be said about your wife?" asked Polk, undiplomatically.

"Yes, but my wife has no history of lurking in the shadows of a treasonous spy organization."

"Returning to my opening question to Mr. Tallifierro," spoke the President, "I am prepared to stick with the team that got us to the dance. With all the investigating that the Bureau and the Agency have done since 9/11/2001, Richmond's team has been the only one to identify our U.S.-based enemies with almost absolute certainty; and to compile persuasive evidence against them." Underwood and Polk could be seen squirming ever so slightly in their chairs.

"Of course," the President continued, this decision is subject to Mr. Tallifierro's presenting a workable plan for preventing the apparent planned terror attack and for destroying HARP or QUEST, or whatever other ridiculous thing they call themselves, in the process.

"Mr. Tallifierro, please proceed to tell us your plan."

"My plan is to penetrate the HARP conspiracy and use sound counterespionage tradecraft to compromise its secrecy and operations. Taking a page out of Angleton's book, we will penetrate the conspiracy at the outer edges and then move inward. I believe we have exposed vulnerability at the periphery of the spy circle which can be exploited. The first is Hajib, born in Islamabad, Pakistan to Pakistani-American parents. He made several suspicious trips to Afghanistan before 9/11, ostensibly on FBI business. From the video, we saw that he is not highly regarded by Spence, the de facto leader. He would appear to be the weakest link. We will try first to turn him, and then to double him. We'll make use of the Philby "Trust method" to establish our credibility with him. He seemed particularly upset by the plan to assassinate me and Douglas Booker and this gives us a real opening.

Because she has volunteered, we will use Clarissa to seek to solidify her renewed relationship with Deidre Wilson, to test Deidre's current intentions. If the Charleston note was an attempt to reach out to escape from the cabal, then we will move in to turn and double her as well. If it goes the other way and she tries to reel Clarissa into the conspiracy, we will exploit that to learn more about HARP's inner workings. If in the process of turning Hajib and Deidre, we find out that our suspicions that Scherzer is also a weak link are valid, then we'll move in on him as well. But we believe our best chance of creating a double-sided agent is with Deidre.

At some point, we'll have to neutralize Q and remove him from the picture completely. The profile we have developed on him is that he is a rock-solid bad guy who can't be redeemed or broken. Therefore, he has to be eliminated."

"What do you mean by eliminated?" asked the President and Director Polk almost simultaneously. "Are you talking about a Bin Laden-type liquidation?" asked Polk. No, not necessarily. Rendition to a maximum security detention facility would probably be just as effective. Hopefully, when all of this is over, he, Spence and the others can be tried for treason, murder, espionage and other high crimes, in Federal Court."

The next target is Spence. Both my father and I believe he was lying when he said he didn't know the target of the next terrorist attack. So does Ben Berger. Ignorance of such a critical detail is not how Spence operates. He's an egomaniacal control freak and obsessive when it comes to details.

Beginning with our research and continuing through close surveillance, we have gotten a pretty good handle on what makes

Spence run. It would be a complete departure from character for him not to know where the attack was going to take place. Three CIA body language experts have also observed his demeanor on the Citadel disk and agree that he was lying.

We need to isolate Spence—make him feel that he is all alone at the top of the pyramid, without allies, and headed towards bearing the major brunt of the consequences from the planned operation. The key to accomplishing that is exposing the other confederates first and then turning them against Spence. Any one or more of them may provide us with valuable information. But given the unpredictability of the plan of attack we have to move fast. But we don't want to move in and arrest Spence until we have him on the ropes. Right now, he might very well lawyer-up and tell us nothing. We first want to be in the position where we can threaten him with having all his confederates testify against him, plus face a possible death penalty. Stage One is to seek to turn and recruit Hajib and Wilson. If that proves successful, we use the same approach with Scherzer. If none of that works, we quickly arrest the three of them plus Kyle Collins and interrogate them. At first we'll leave Spence out there all alone. We want him to feel threatened and isolated enough to at least call off the attack. After giving him a short window of opportunity to do that, we'll take him into custody for interrogation."

"Why don't we just run them all in now?" asked Polk.

"Because that won't necessarily prevent the attack."

"Well what makes you so sure your complex plan will stop it?" Polk was obviously no fan of Rick.

"I'm not. I just think it's the best chance we have. Of course, no matter what, Homeland Security will continue working nonstop to thwart the attack."

"That's a given," observed Underwood.

"And what about the risks of using your wife?" continued Polk, unabashed. She has no professional training and no security clearance."

"Well the same thing could be said of the vast majority of our agents across the globe."

"But no matter what you say," continued Polk heatedly, "you can't guarantee the total loyalty of your wife."

"Intelligence and counterintelligence are not about guarantees," retorted Rick, "they are about probabilities of success versus failure."

"Well I believe your plan has a low probability of success."

"I don't," said the President, casting the only vote that counted. "Begin implementing your plan today."

Chapter Fifteen

THE BATTLE IS JOINED

Q considered himself to be in better physical shape than 99% of all the 78-year olds in the world. As he passed most other joggers on his favorite route through Georgetown's Rock Creek Park, his sense of wellbeing on this particularly lovely spring morning was at its peak. The plans made in Charleston were sound and gave him something to look forward to. He hadn't felt so exhilarated since watching the Twin Towers fall and crumble on 9/11/01. Life was good. Of course there were discordant notes at the Citadel meeting. Spence had optimized his inside coup and was now clearly the undisputed leader of Quest. But Q surprised himself by feeling no envy or resentment. After all, Spence was his son, whose success was a source of great paternal pride. And more importantly, at age 58, Spence was better suited to handle the rigors of Quest's militant program than he was.

More irritating was the spinelessness of Hajib and Scherzer. They were lily-livered bureaucrats of the kind Q had always taken great joy in purging from his organizations. But as he spoke these words aloud he could feel his blood pressure rising. That was not good. He quickly tamped down his anger by switching his thoughts elsewhere. He was pleased that his son had come down hard on Hajib even though the Pakistani-American was the one who had introduced them in 1996 to the bin Laden family. He was particularly proud of Spence for having agreed to move Collins into the inner circle. His promotion, together with trimming some of the fat, would make Quest leaner and meaner. He would recommend to his son that Deidre be promoted as well. This thought melted away his annoyance at the candy-assed runners up ahead who were beginning to slow down and bunch up as they approached the M Street Tunnel.

Q's fervent desire beyond the destruction of the West was to build an all-family business. It was this thought which impassioned and consumed him. Deidre's promotion would be a clear positive.

*   *   *

Rick believed Clarissa when she explained that she knew her father was in a nefarious business but just not which one. When her parents were still together she would pick up words and fragments of sentences here and there when he would remove himself to a different room to talk to his cohorts; or when he was on the phone. Considering how successful Paul Spence had been with the growth of HARP (Quest), he was surprisingly indiscreet. Was this a product of his arrogance? She thought so. It ran in the family—in her younger brother and older sister also; but not in her mother, who while shallow and materialistic, was also gentle and considerate. Clarissa credited her for whatever redeeming grace had been preserved in the Spence offspring. These thoughts were interesting to Clarissa but also distracting and she had no time for them now. She had to get ready to meet Deidre.

*   *   *

At about the same time Henry Hajib, after keeping Black and

Mineo waiting in his outer office for a half hour, allowed them in his private office but without greeting them or shaking hands. His contemptuous attitude changed after they played a segment of the Citadel Video for him:

"And while you're at it, take care of Booker too..."

"No problem."

"Okay, will you put out the work order?"

"Oh, look," said Mineo, "that's you Mr. Hajib getting up and leaving the room. Gee, you don't look so hot. It must have been those fried grits you had for breakfast at the Citadel Mess." They had now gotten his attention and Hajib was scared.

Fifteen minutes later Black's Buick Sedan carried the three men across the Sixteenth Street Bridge, headed for Langley. Hajib sat in the back seat with his arms folded and made no protest.

*   *   *

An alarm sounded in Q's brain. Its screeching noise was a product of his imagination only, though it might as well have been real for it produced in Q an equivalent uneasiness. His instincts signaled danger. The bunched up runners further ahead in the tunnel suddenly stopped, pivoted and shouted, "FBI," and ordered Q to get down on the ground face first—hands behind his back.

"Go fuck yourselves," was Q's response. He had faced worse many times in the sixties and seventies in street fights in the back alleys of Berlin. But now the odds were bad. Six agents blocked his way, including Fasbender and some female. But he would not surrender. Backpedaling quickly, he was able to keep an eye on his pursuers in case some of them got trigger-happy. He wasn't really worried. They wanted him alive; otherwise he'd already be dead. He would backpedal until he reached the tunnel opening. To keep them from rushing him he pulled a stiletto from his sock and pointed it menacingly at the agents. Perhaps aware of Q's reputation as a premier knife fighter, the agents were content to approach him at the same pace as his reverse movement. Q allowed himself a quick turn of his head to see how far he was from the opening; it was still close to a hundred feet but his pursuers were slowly narrowing the gap. He did some quick calculations which told him that unless they quickened their pace they would not be on him until he backed through the opening. He'd worry about what might await him on the other side when he got there. He hated U.S. government agents for their cocksuredness and arrogance. He would love to take one of them down with his knife. But it might put an end to him too and he eagerly wanted to stick around long enough to witness the next attack on one of America's cities, not an act of terrorism to him, rather another noble action in a just war.

He eyed the female. The bitch had her weapon in firing position and no sign of fear or awareness of her natural gender-inferiority showed on her face. He could never respect a country that allowed women to do men's jobs and especially women with no sense of modesty or humility. The Muslims got it right. Let the lesser gender cover themselves in public. Western women were shameless and deserved to be punished.

Could he take her down, at what was now about twenty feet, with his knife? A splendid and savage toss getting her right between the eyes would be glorious. He'd have to throw underhand because if he lifted the knife, they would shoot him before he could get the throw off. But he was confident he could get an underhand toss off before they opened fire. His aim might be slightly askew but at the very worst he would get her in the neck or chest. What a splendid way that would be for him to exit this mortal coil!

Q again gauged the distance and angle. They were now only about fifteen feet away, making the throw even easier. He was sure he could make it. Joy mixed with excitement as he continued to backpedal and tighten his hand on the knife. The entire purpose of his existence had distilled itself into this singular moment. But it had to be now. He had allowed himself to be distracted and the tunnel opening was right behind him...one last quick aim and...two powerful arms enveloped Q in a bear hug from behind.

He could not move. It was over. He barely noticed the FBI agents cuffing him from behind. All he could see was a guy he remembered from the Company, Dubinsky—with blacksmith's arms—laughing at him. And the final humiliation. The female giving him his Miranda warnings. For Ellie Hirsch it was the high point of her career. For Q the low point of his life.

$$* \quad * \quad *$$

Casa Felicia in Foggy Bottom, only a block from the Watergate Complex, was one of DC's finest Italian Restaurants. It was also Clarissa's choice for her dinner with Deidre. The superb Northern Italian cuisine and an excellent wine list would be pleasing to Deidre; and the dimly lit ambiance, including soft instrumental music, would be conducive to the type of relaxed conversation Clarissa had in mind.

After their main course, while each of them was sipping an Expresso, Clarissa broached the subject which they both knew was the real reason for the dinner.

"Deidre, I know you and I have not always gotten along but I have always loved you and now I am very worried about you."

"Oh, and why is that?" Clarissa could hear the false bravado in Deidre's voice.

"First, to keep this conversation confidential and privileged, I want you to hire me right now as your lawyer."

"You're hired counselor."

"Okay, the answer to your question is, because you are far too involved with Dad and Grandpa in their business."

"What business is that?"

"You know what business I'm talking about. Dad has been slowly going off the deep end since we were teenagers. Now, any chance of his changing course is gone. He has been exposed and he's going down and I'm afraid he'll drag you down with him."

Clarissa's blunt openness triggered an anti-American diatribe by

Deidre which continued for a good ten minutes. Significantly, however, Deidre never once raised her voice. Clarissa took Deidre's self-control as a signal that her sister was still concerned about self-preservation, and that her rant flowed from parental conditioning rather than conviction.

Clarissa had just listened quietly without interrupting while Deidre vented her resentment and angst. Finally she brought her diatribe to a close and stared silently at Clarissa, but with anxiety etched on her face.

After the waiter brought two Zambucccas on the rocks, Deidre spoke again, but this time with sorrow rather than anger.

"I was hard at work on my Masters at Columbia on 9/11 and knew nothing about the back story. I don't even think Scherzer or Hajib were in the loop as to the 9/11 attack, and I certainly wasn't. I think the whole thing was facilitated by Dad and Grandpa. They were hired by Osama bin Laden and Zawahiri, his chief deputy. It was by his skillful management of the New York logistics of the attack that Dad proved his mettle once and for all with Al Qaeda's upper echelon. For the first time bin Laden came across with some real money to fund Quest's mission. It was after the U.N. bombing that Dad recruited me to spy on Burns and Crowe. It's a good thing Booker and the President brought Rick in to investigate because Burns' official investigation was totally compromised from the start."

"Grandpa wants me brought into the inner circle together with that despicable Kyle Collins, who I believe has been their henchman for years. I keep putting them off but pretty soon they are going to get suspicious. I'm really frightened Clarissa!"

"Let me ask you a question as your lawyer rather than your sister. Has Quest ever divulged the details of any of their operations to you?"

"No."

"Thank God for that. If they had and you did nothing to report them to the authorities, you could have been facing a long prison term."

"Tell me what to do, sis," pleaded Deidre with pain in her voice.

"As soon as we finish our drinks and settle the tab, you and I are leaving this place. But you're not going home. We're taking a cab to meet with Rick. He'll be calling the shots from now on. But one last question, did you arrange for me to find the note about Quest's mission?"

"Yes, call it a cry for help."

"That's also good news. It should count in your favor."

"I'm really in trouble, aren't I?"

"If you knew nothing about the terrorism in advance you may still be okay."

"Shouldn't I be packing a bag or something?"

Clarissa hesitated. She didn't want to reveal too much. "No, I'll pick up whatever you need." Privately, Clarissa was terrified for her sister.

*   *   *

Rick's shuffling of his team to carve out a temporary unit composed of Chris Berger, Stan Dubinsky and Cynthia Torres, to pursue Scherzer, turned out to be a case of overkill. Within twenty-four hours after Hajib had been shipped—purportedly in secret—to an isolated holding cell in a dungeon-like wing of CIA Headquarters, FBI Deputy Director Clyde Underwood received a phone call from Scherzer's high-powered Washington lawyer. His client, Congressman Mark Scherzer, was willing to cooperate fully in return for not being taken into custody, but rather being interviewed at the lawyer's office. Underwood listened politely and then calmly told the attorney that his client had one hour to present himself at the closest field office of the FBI to be placed under arrest. Underwood did add that in return for Scherzer's surrender within the allotted time and his full cooperation thereafter, Underwood would refrain from notifying the media.

*   *   *

Sunday morning, Rick gazed out onto the Potomac from his elevated deck. He worked nonstop these days and today was not a time out for "R and R." He set his mind in review mode. So far, all was going according to plan. Hajib was the first to crack, spewing a line of self-serving crap. Coached by his talented lawyer from Williams and Connolly, the crackerjack firm founded by the late Edward Bennett Williams, Hajib was spilling his guts to the Special Prosecutor appointed by the Justice Department—spinning his mea culpas to maximize the culpability of Spence and Q—while minimizing his own.

The President had demanded Hajib be fired the same day he was escorted by Black and Mineo to Langley. He also appointed Clyde Underwood as Acting Director of the FBI immediately after firing Flaherty.

Scherzer had also turned state's evidence. He had made bail and was in witness protection. Congressional impeachment proceedings were underway.

A warrant had been issued for Spence's arrest. But no one was really trying to arrest him. With Underwood's cooperation, Rick had turned Deidre, made her a double-sided woman and sent her in, undercover, to join Spence. Feeling trapped and isolated, Spence was more than eager to have his daughter at his side. He was under heavy surveillance, abetted by Deidre's frequent and risky phone calls to Rick to keep him apprised of their location.

The clever Kyle Collins remained at liberty. He was always too smart to allow any overt connection between himself and the core group of Quest. Rick did not have the evidence to arrest him, even though both Spence and Collins were under twenty-four-hour surveillance. What bothered Rick was not that Spence and Collins were still out there. He needed one or both of them to be the bridge to the terrorists and wouldn't take them in even if he could. What worried him was that Collins would see through Deidre's masquerade. Then Clarissa's sister, whom she had always loved, would be in grave danger. So would the United States of America.

Burns was seemingly clueless as to what had happened to Deidre. He was savvy enough to be highly suspicious of Rick's possible involvement, but had nothing solid to go on. In the final analysis, he didn't really care that much. His only real concern was about the bad publicity that would follow if his relationship with Deidre became public.

*   *   *

The President was under extraordinary stress. The planned attack was worse than the metaphorical ticking time bomb. That would be nerve wracking enough. But what made this a quantum leap beyond the countdown to an explosion was the fact that they knew neither when the bomb would go off, nor where.

Rick was equally stressed but his comparative youth gave him the resources to withstand it better than the President. It was pretty amazing when you got right down to it. Upon Rick's shoulders were the planning and implementation of the counteroffensive, the management and supervision of his ten-agent team, the integration of the various parts of the U.S. initiative to thwart the attack; and his serving as sole communicator of events to the President.

This last task meant he had to tolerate National Security Director Polk's constant demands for new information and his incessant interference. But he knew now that Clarissa was innocent. His reaffirmation of faith in her and in himself would see them through, at least that was his fervent hope.

Chapter Sixteen

APOCALYPSE WHEN?

Rick's counteroffensive was stalled; his engine flooded. All the pieces were in place but the disclosures from Hajib, Scherzer and Deidre Wilson had yielded nothing as to the how, where or when of the attack. Polk, Underwood and the President got the same alerts from NSA and Homeland Security that he did—infuriatingly vague and ominous warnings of imminent attack. The president had raised the threat level to Defcon 4.

Polk was frantic, Underwood was grim and the President was alarmingly mute. Unbeknownst to Rick, Polk remonstrated with the President daily to have Rick removed and his operation absorbed into the overall Homeland Security effort, with Underwood and Burns as the new co-leaders of Rick's unit. But Rick didn't need to know the details of Polk's effort to preempt him. He knew instinctively that if he didn't make a break-through soon, he would be standing with one foot out the door and the other on a banana peel.

Under heavy interrogation, Q had yielded nothing. Deidre was right that Scherzer and Hajib had been kept ignorant of any details of the planned attacks and the network which would carry it out. That left Collins. Rick got at least two calls a day from Polk pressuring him to arrest and interrogate Collins. And he would have but for the fact that Deidre was getting close.

Each day Spence involved her more and more in his affairs. She now was in charge of payroll and would hand envelopes full of cash to any number of strange individuals to whom Spence granted access to the house he shared with Deidre.

But following the money trail would not necessarily lead to the heart of the conspiracy. There would be multiple levels of cut-outs between the cash delivery and its ultimate destination.

The only person Rick wanted to hear from right now was Deidre. He ordered his secretary to hold all calls for the next hour except hers. He needed uninterrupted time to think; and fifty minutes into the hour he was no closer to a breakthrough. But then as if the wish gave birth to the event, Deidre's hot line began to blink.

"Deidre?"

"Rick, listen carefully. I'm in a cab on the way to meet my father and Kyle for dinner. Kyle is very suspicious of me, and I'm scared. I don't have time to explain. I want you to write down exactly what I read to you. It was on my father's private server that only he has access to. It's an email he sent yesterday, to a recipient named 'Game-DayFantasyFootball@verizon.net'. Do you have something to write with?"

"Yes, shoot."

"Okay, here goes."

"Victory"

"The forsaken heart yearns for solace; the abandoned island offers none;

```
But on a melancholy cruise to the
City of Twos my spirits soared to
the heights;

At vision's peak I made my mark;
pledged to follow my fate;

And soon I'll embark on a noble
steed to the path that clings to the
sea;

Where by God's angry fist and my
steadfast faith I'll lay claim to
victory."
```

*   *   *

"Is that a paper copy you're reading from?"

"Yes"

"Where did you get it?"

"In my father's safe. He gave me the combination so I could take out cash for the pay-offs."

"I don't have to ask if you put the original back, do I?"

"No, you don't have to ask."

"Does anyone other than you and Spence have the combination?"

"I don't think so."

"Okay, where are you going for dinner?"

"I don't know. I'm supposed to go to a rest stop on the George Washington Parkway, where they'll pick me up. The Alexandria stop, but I'm to meet them there in only three minutes."

"Deidre, listen to me. This is critical. Don't eat or drink anything. Make up some excuse. You need to fast because of lab tests you're having bright and early tomorrow; or you had a double root canal this afternoon. Anything you're comfortable with. You're a pro, so give them a plausible excuse."

"Copy that. I have to hang up. We're almost at the rest stop."

Rick was his typical cool under pressure. He had taken the poem down in shorthand and now wrote it out on a yellow pad in clear cursive. He read it again. There could be no doubt. It was code. An eerie feeling came over him. He already had deciphered it in his own mind and wondered why it was so easy...but maybe it's not...maybe I'm wrong in my translation. The multiple possibilities buzzed in his brain. Was it a plant which Spence wanted found? Was his deciphering correct and Spence just made it simple to deceive them into thinking it was a hoax, when in fact it was genuine? Or was the code far more complex than it seemed at first blush?

"Enough of this crap! I'm not a cryptologist. I need the professionals here to decipher this thing," argued Rick to himself, as he pushed the intercom button. "Mort, call The Crypt and get the A Team up here stat!"

*   *   *

Mort Fasbender had come to know Richmond Tallifierro better than anyone—even Rick's father—but this was not uncommon among war buddies. Of course, Rick and Mort were actually civilians, but that was a mere technicality. Make no mistake, they were soldiers. Soldiers upon whose shoulders countless lives and the security of the nation rested.

The "Crypt" was the nickname for the CIA Cryptology Center, with camouflaged offices at the end of a long, dimly lit corridor, to which Fasbender now sprinted. He wasn't going to leave anything to chance. Rick's command required his personal attention. He would not leave the selection of the cryptologists to someone else and wasn't going to settle for any lesser talents, just because the top guys were busy.

His mission was a success and he personally accompanied the three most highly regarded post 9/11 cryptologists to Rick's office. Rick's stress was palpable and the least Mort could do was to make sure he had only the best men available to him. And to make sure no one ran low on fuel, he had the secretaries take lunch orders for the five of them.

Before providing a copy of the cryptic writing to each man, Rick swore them to secrecy and briefed them on the facts of the crisis, but only to the extent of what they needed to know. He also stressed to them the urgency of their assignment and that he wanted them to decipher the message on the basis of not only the words themselves but also the context in which they were written. He informed them that NSA had advised that Game-DayFantasyFootball@verizon.net was a cover website and email address for a group serving as a communications intermediary. A cut-out, used by criminal enterprises to insulate themselves from detection. It had no political affiliations, and was strictly in it for profit.

Rick separated the three experts, assigning each to a vacant office. He gave them a time limit of one hour. They were not to converse during that time. Each would decode the message independently. At the end of an hour he dispatched Fasbender to collect them and bring them back to Rick's office to hand-in and defend their decoding reports. They were also instructed to give their reasoning before their conclusion.

The senior cryptologist, Bruce Balaban, was asked to report first. He prefaced his substantive comments by stating that after his first reading of the message he had jotted down the names of eight cities which arguably could, based on the message, be targets: New York, Miami, Chicago, Seattle, San Diego, Los Angeles, New Orleans and San Francisco. After several more readings he wrote down the various clues and matched each one up with identifying characteristics of the cities:

> "abandoned island"—San Francisco (Alcatraz, though not technically abandoned)

> "the city of twos"—1. San Francisco (two major bridges);

2. New York (Manhattan and Brooklyn).

"heights"—1. San Francisco (Pacific Heights)

2. New York (Washington Heights)

"divided in two"—1. New York (Divided by the East River)

2. San Francisco (Divided by the Divisidero)

"mark"—San Fran (St. Mark Hotel)

"embark"—San Fran (The Embarcadero)

"Path that clings to the sea"—could refer to a characteristic of all 8 cities.

"noble steed"—San Fran (could refer to a cable car)

"the forsaken heart"—San Francisco ("I left my heart in San Francisco")

Conclusion: San Francisco

Neither Balaban's conclusion nor the fact that the other two cryptologists came to the same conclusion was a surprise to Rick. He concurred on the basis of just one quick reading.

The cryptologists were dismissed so Rick and Mort could brainstorm the problem. Both agonized over the seemingly obvious code. Mort was especially beset by doubts but he wasn't aware of all the data Rick had received within the last couple of hours.

"Mort, you need to know that NSA has reported unusually heavy phone and email chatter in the Bay area. And one of my most trustworthy CI's has told us that Collins registered in a hotel in Oakland within the last hour. Our own surveillance people have reported that Spence and Deidre just boarded a flight from Reno to

San Jose. But, this only confirmed what I already knew." Mort
didn't ask how he knew.

"But all of this same info would have gone to Collins at National
Intelligence. How do we know that they haven't changed the
target?" asked Mort.

"Because the same day that the President and Polk saw the
Citadel video, Collins was fired, physically removed by Security
from the O.D.N.I. building with only the clothes on his back. His
access to O.D.N.I. was revoked and his security clearance lifted."

"I don't know," said Fasbender, "the whole thing still has the
feel of a ruse."

"Maybe" said Rick. "Anyway let's meet again in an hour." Mort
looked like he had more on his mind but left anyway. Rick gazed
out the window of his office but saw nothing. Mort's doubts were
fully justified. But how could he not identify San Francisco as the
target? The circumstantial evidence was strong. The consequences
of not acting aggressively could be catastrophic. He had to act on the
basis of the evidence he had, not the evidence he didn't have.

In Deidre he had an undercover agent in place. How many other
opportunities had presented themselves with this type of proximity
to the core? It was classic espionage. He was convinced that in post
9/11 America, classic intelligence tradecraft had been grossly
undervalued. Polk was a prime example. His idea of intelligence
was high-tech drones and satellites, supplemented by a small army
of CIA paramilitary types who would pull in all the usual suspects
and interrogate them, rendition-style, in cold warehouses—until they
talked. To Rick's mind this was not only corrosive of the character
of America but inefficient as well. Contrary to Hollywood's version,
Osama bin Laden was not found because an al Qaeda operative
revealed his location under torture, but rather as a result of years of
good old fashion pavement pounding and sound espionage
techniques—those used so successfully by Elliott and Angleton; and
the other side who used the low-tech methodology of Philby, their
mentor.

But before he called the President, Rick wanted just one more piece of corroborating evidence. He had to take the risk of possibly putting Deidre in jeopardy. If not now, when? He picked up the dedicated cell phone and texted a message in code to her: "Who won the World Series last year?" This was code for, "Is N.Y. the target?" The seconds ticked away. Rick was surprisingly calm and confident. He knew that after all these months, the end game was near. And intuitively he believed San Francisco was where it would be played.

Five minutes passed, then ten, then fifteen but he was not impatient. A case-officer must make a leap of faith to a belief in his agent. Otherwise he has no business sending her out. His patience was rewarded because nineteen minutes after texting, his cellphone sounded the musical alert for an incoming text message. Rick read it: "Not sure but it wasn't New York. f.y.i. Marin's cool."

Marin County was directly across San Francisco Bay from the majestic city. Rick picked up his office phone and punched the speed dial for the office of the President of the United States.

Chapter Seventeen

PUSH-BACK

NSA intercepts of phone calls, resulting from FISA Court Warrants, were—upon Polk's new orders—not only provided to Rick but also to the National Security Council. Rick had no problem with that; but when a copy of a memo from Polk to the President landed on Rick's desk, calling for the assimilation of his investigative team into the Clandestine Division of the CIA, Rick seethed with anger. This bureaucratic bullshit had to stop. He didn't need this distraction. Not when a national crisis demanded every ounce of energy and attention he could muster. "Just let me do my damn job," he beseeched the portrait of Wild Bill Donovan, founder of the O.S.S., hanging on his office wall. "Wild Bill" offered no consolation. He would resign in a heart beat, but under the circumstances, that would be a cowardly act of self-pity and a betrayal of trust. No, he'd just keep doing his job as best he could for as long as the President still wanted him.

The intercepts were encrypted and he needed to run them down to the Crypt asap. Balaban and his two colleagues were now working successive eight hour shifts to provide instant responses, 24/7. The two not on duty were on call, subject to returning to duty on five minutes' notice.

*   *   *

Fasbender returned after exactly sixty minutes. The instant he walked into Rick's office, he noticed something different about him.

It wasn't a mood shift so much as a different aura. The man he left one hour before was as tight as a drum with care lines etched in his face. But the new version of the chief radiated confidence and self-assuredness.

"Mort, sit down, pour yourself a whiskey if you want."

"No thanks, boss. I don't want my senses to be chemically altered even in the slightest."

"Well, I have good news and bad news. First the good: Since the U.N. attack I have had a team of counterterrorism specialists patrolling and monitoring the border between Northern Idaho and British Columbia. After the Millennium, Booker's Counterterrorism people were able to identify a three-mile stretch along the border where a team of Al Qaeda infiltrators managed to cross into U.S. territory with the intention of attacking LAX, during L.A.'s Millennium celebrations. Earlier today our team captured two suspected Jihadists within seconds of crossing the same stretch of border. One of them was carrying a map of San Francisco. Highlighted were Fisherman's Wharf, Coit Tower, The Transamerica Pyramid, The Golden Gate Bridge, the Bay Bridge, the Embarcadero.

Each of them carried a collapsible shoulder-fired missile launcher.

"So what's the bad news?"

"The bad news is that Deidre and Spence have checked out of their San Jose Hotel and we've lost them at least temporarily."

"What about Collins?"

"Still in Oakland. And I've given orders to our counterterrorism team in the Bay Area to arrest him."

"I thought you didn't have the evidence?"

"I didn't then. I do now. Two new developments rise to the level of overt acts in furtherance of a RICO Criminal Conspiracy. First, the Defense Intelligence Agency—using a FISA warrant—intercepted a phone call between Collins and Abu Ata, the suspected mastermind of the aborted Millennium attack in 2000, in which they agreed to meet in a Monterrey café catering to Middle Easterners. Second, Balaban decrypted an NSA intercept of an email between Collins and Spence, the day before the arrests at the border. During their conversation, Spence told Collins that their friends from Montreal would be arriving the next day in San Francisco on a sightseeing trip."

"I wasn't aware you were so well versed in Criminal Law, Rick."

"I'm not, smartass, but I happen to be married to our unit's attorney, who is."

The exchange was the first moment of levity the two friends had allowed themselves in months.

"We sent agents to Monterey to pick up Abu Ata as well but he was apparently tipped off and didn't show up for his meet with Collins."

"I can't begin to tell you all the things Homeland Security is doing to protect San Francisco, but some of them are, checking every cargo container in the Seaport; suspending all flights into San Fran International for at least the next week...suspending train arrivals as well...scrambling fighter planes at regular intervals during that time frame; setting up FBI and State Police road checks on all thoroughfares into the city; massive internments of all suspected terrorists and persons of interest. The entire San Francisco and Oakland Police Departments are on duty until further notice—all days off and vacations cancelled. Foreign flight into the rest of the U.S. will not be stopped—except for flights originating in countries on the O.D.N.I.'s list of 'terrorist-source' nations. Five thousand

FBI, ATF, CIA, Customs, DIA and NSA agents and another thousand State and City internal security agents are already on the ground in the Bay Area, or will be within the next few hours."

"The White House and NSC have tasked us with an intelligence role exclusively. They have left the shape and scope of it up to us. And the President has relieved Polk of his duties. Doug Booker is back, as Acting Director of the NSC for the duration of the crisis."

"Apparently the two hostiles captured at the border have talked, naming Mohammed Abdul Aziz as their chief and have described a planned terrorist attack this week on San Francisco, involving an army of Jihadist infiltrators from Mexico, Canada and the Middle East, employing a multitude of weapons and tactics, including anthrax, bombs, AR-15 assault rifles, poison for the city's water supply and chemical weapons."

"One hundred of the enemy combatants are said to be armed with shoulder-fired RPGs. There will be suicide bombers, demolition experts and bomb-equipped vehicles. Strict orders from their leadership, which includes al Qaeda and ISIS, are to never surrender and to fight to the death."

"If our job is strictly intelligence, why aren't we out in the field trawling for sources and picking up leads on the status of enemy operations?"

"We are Mort but you're not. You're more valuable to me here at Centcom. We have learned from I.N.S. that our porous border with Canada, and to a lesser extent with Mexico, has been leaking hostiles onto U.S. soil for weeks, with large numbers of commando trained guerillas surrounding and penetrating the Bay areas, where Jihadist sleeper cells are hiding them. The Pentagon, ATF and FBI are in the final stages of formulating plans to move in on them en masse. The enemy is said to be concentrated in clusters which will make our job easier. But there will be civilian casualties."

"Within the next several hours we'll be getting reports from the various intelligence people on the ground as to the locations of the attackers. I'll need your help in evaluating the intelligence quickly

and synthesizing it so we can give coherent reports to the Army's
G-2 in Santa Cruz. There, Army Rangers, Navy Seals and Delta
Force Commandos are awaiting orders to move in."

*   *   *

United Flight 501 put down at Sacramento. Kyle Collins was
supposed to meet and pick-up Spence and Deidre at the airport but
was a no-show. They had no way of knowing however, that the
reason for his non-appearance was that he was locked up in a cell in
the basement of the Federal District Courthouse in San Francisco,
awaiting arraignment on charges of treason, espionage and criminal
enterprise. While he waited, FBI counterintelligence specialists were
having a field day interrogating him.

*   *   *

With Rick and Mort ensconced in headquarters for the
foreseeable future, Rick again realigned his teams. He designated
Ben Berger as Field Coordinator of the agent teams. Dubinsky was
now paired with Ellie Hirsch; Cynthia Torres with Chris Berger and
Walter Black with Joe Mineo. Rick would have preferred a fourth
team that he could assign to the South Beach District of the city; but
he had Ben Berger there and had to trust that Ben's overall brilliance
would be enough.

Dubinsky and Hirsch were assigned to the Presidio and Marina
Districts; Torres and Berger to the Inner Mission District; Black and
Mineo to Bayview, Hunters Point and Candlestick Point. All teams
were to liaise with their FBI counterparts. Ben Berger was assigned
three FBI Agents to work under his supervision. As the lead team
their job was to rove to other districts of the city as needed. Golden
Gate and Lincoln Parks were of particular concern. But the heavy
presence of Navy Seal teams in the Lake Shore area accompanied by
a Naval Intelligence Detachment made it less of a concern.

Delta Force accompanied by an Army Intelligence Detachment
had primary responsibility for the City of Oakland. And a regiment

of Army Rangers was being held in reserve, to be deployed wherever conditions on the ground dictated it.

*   *   *

Dubinsky and Hirsch drove east in their rental car on Marina Boulevard along the bay, toward the Golden Gate Bridge. Ellie slowed and pulled into a parking area abutting an idyllic public park on their right. The park was actually an open green on the bay with a splendid view of the bridge in the distance. The main occupants were children at play, mothers, one or two fathers and a host of child-care workers—some in white uniforms. Benches were dispersed throughout but were sparsely occupied. Hirsch and Dubinsky picked out a bench in the shade and headed toward it. It was only wide enough for three adults and a nattily dressed but painfully thin man of about fifty sat squarely in the middle. A pair of eye glasses tied to a lanyard around his neck, lay against his chest. He made no attempt to move in order to allow them to sit next to each other, so they sat, one on either side of him. After about five minutes of silence, Dubinsky spoke:

"Is that today's newspaper?"

"Yes."

"Are you done with it?"

"Yes, nothing but scandal and corruption anyway," he said, as he handed the newspaper to Dubinsky.

"Much obliged."

The phrase, "nothing but scandal and corruption anyway" were the code words which established the man's bona fides. He was without a doubt Agent 11932421, the legendary spy who had exposed and thereby prevented the planned Bicentennial attacks in 2000. A surge of excitement charged through both Dubinsky and Hirsch, triggered by anticipation over what the contents of the folded newspaper would reveal.

A shot rang out; Agent 11932421 slumped down with a bullet from a high-powered rifle leaving a hole between his eyes. The next shot shattered the wood of the backrest, where Hirsch had sat only a split second before.

Her instinctual movement upon hearing the first shot had saved her life. Before a third shot was fired, Hirsch and Dubinsky were on the ground. The third shot hit Dubinsky in the left shoulder. He and Hirsch scrambled around the bench and lay flat behind it. Fourth, fifth and sixth shots harmlessly shattered the wood of the bench seat and backrest.

Chaos reigned—children screaming and running in every direction—adults dropping ice cream cones, paperback books, cans of soda. Shouting their charges' names, they raced after them in a panic. Dubinsky sighted a muzzle flash on the fifth shot and emptied his 45 caliber revolver into a copse of trees about 200 feet distant. There were no further shots. He handed the blood-spattered newspaper to Hirsch and they ran, crouched-down, back to the car. CIA Agent 11932421 had become the first fatality of the only ground invasion by a foreign power on United States soil since the War of 1812.

*   *   *

Fasbender got some welcome help from Tom Tallifierro with receiving and responding to the large volumn of messages and pleas now pouring into Centcom. One of the most urgent was from Agent Ellie Hirsch reporting that Agent Dubinsky had been wounded in a shoot out. An ambulance was on its way to take him to the hospital but Hirsch would not be accompanying him. It was, she said, of the greatest urgency that she return to the makeshift headquarters Berger had set up at Jackson Square. She wouldn't say why. Since Rick was on the radio hook-up with the G-2 nonstop, Mort took it on his own authority to dispatch an armed team to pick her up. Later, when Rick and Mort read the contents of what Hirsch transmitted to them, the wisdom of Mort's decision was crystal clear.

*   *   *

Back at Langley, Rick's reception staff was startled when their door swung open abruptly and a group of armed, tough-looking men and women with weapons drawn, burst through. CIA junior agent Meredith Kerr bravely drew her weapon and stood ready to defend her unit. It was hardly necessary because in the center of the group was an elderly gentleman in suit and tie with gentle eyes and a studious look about him.

"I'm Douglas Booker; here to see Agent-in-Charge, Tallifierro." Hearing the commotion, Tom Tallifierro emerged from an inner office. His face broke out in a grin as the secret service agents cleared the way for him to approach and embrace his friend and colleague of almost fifty ears.

After the warm greeting, Tom escorted Booker into Rick's office.

"I'm surprised to see you Mr. Director, but you know you're always welcome wherever there's a member of the Tallifierro family," said Rick.

"I know that and I apologize for the unannounced visit and inelegant entrance. Given the assassination threat against both you and I, the Secret Service has been ordered by POTUS to protect his new acting Director of National Security at all costs. The niceties of courtesy have been lost in the shuffle."

Booker went on to explain that the President wanted his own man, Booker, in Langley at the eye of the storm.

What triggered all this was the folded 10 x 15 map delivered inside the newspaper by Agent 11932421 to Dubinsky and Hirsch. Within five minutes after receiving transmittal of the map from Hirsch, Rick had sent copies through secret channels to the G-2 in Santa Cruz, the Commander of Combined Forces for the Bay Area Operation, The President, Booker and the Chairman of the Joint Chiefs of Staff. The map was enlarged to show all of the streets of San Francisco and environs. Each circle drawn on the map in red ink denoted the location of a hidden cluster of hostiles. Within perhaps a half hour they expected to learn the real value of the map, for ten minutes before Booker's arrival, a widely dispersed army of FBI and ATF agents, CIA paramilitaries, Seals, Rangers and Delta Force Commandos had moved in on designated target areas. A virtual armada of helicopters hovered above the advancing military and non-military personnel.

Hirsch was back in the Marina District with a replacement partner. The combat units' orders directed them to a location within a couple of blocks of the target clusters. At each of ten locations throughout the city a battalion of elite commandos connected by prearrangement with one of Rick's ten operatives out in the neighborhoods, including the four FBI intelligence specialists conscripted into service for a temporary (yet vital) role.

Ben Berger stayed behind at the Jackson Square headquarters with a couple of body guards to monitor all intelligence operations and to serve as their central command. His second task was to leave open an audio channel with General Vincent Ortega, the Chief of Combat Operations.

At each rendezvous point, an intelligence operative wearing head phones was to direct the combat units to the specific location of the target cluster, kept current by communications from Berger. He would in turn receive the latest locations of the hostile groups from Rick on the other side of the country.

Rick now had access to the best technology America had to offer. His offices included a new war room containing banks of monitors, computers, radar and jumbo screen televisions with live imaging of all target locations.

American troops plus a division of Canadian commandos were set to launch at 1400 hours (1700, East Coast time). Every combat assault would be synchronized to the second. Optimum coordination was deemed essential to minimizing civilian casualties.

In the war room Rick sat gazing at the multiple screens. The centrally positioned table at which he sat was equipped with swivel chairs so that he could quickly adjust his sight-line. To his right sat Tom Tallifierro; to his left Doug Booker. As the seconds ticked down from 13:59 Pacific time to zero hour, almost every person in the room was seized by a paralyzing tension. An exception was Mort Fasbender who moved from post to post confirming instructions and spurring the technicians on with encouraging fist bumps, thumbs-up gestures and "Atta boys"—sprinkled with "stay frosty" and "stay focused." Many in the room would be called upon to make split-second decisions of life or death.

*   *   *

When the balloon went up, the terrorist cluster groups were caught by surprise. They were also outmanned, outgunned and outmaneuvered...had no time to deploy their missile launchers and other assault weapons. With the precision of a SWAT Team, the U.S. units moved in so quickly that the only defense most of the insurgents were able to mount was with handguns.

The terrorists had chosen empty warehouses as their operational launch sites and for the most part were quickly surrounded and contained. Those who made it out into the streets were cut down by sniper fire and U.S. combat assault teams. Yet given their nature, few surrendered. The vast majority fought to the death. Even those contained within the warehouses chose a spirited defense over surrender. Assaults upon the contained terrorists continued throughout the day and night and into the following morning.

Rick implored Ben Berger to adamantly demand of the combat leaders that as many captives as possible be taken. Berger, in turn, pleaded with General Ortega to give the Jihadists a chance to surrender before demolishing them en masse. "Getting vital intelligence through interrogation is essential to our defense against the next offensive," was the essence of Berger's plea.

Berger's entreaties to Ortega and other field officers were only partially successful. Nevertheless, by the time most of the heavy fighting ended at about 1100 hours, roughly twenty-three hours after the U.S. Assault began, Army, Navy, FBI and CIA counterintelligence units were busy interrogating close to a hundred prisoners, including wounded captives whose injuries were not so serious as to prevent them from being questioned.

Meanwhile, each individual officer in charge of a counterintelligence team received a direct phone call from Richmond Tallifierro who they knew was the President's overall Chief of Counterinsurgency operations, demanding that detailed interrogation reports be electronically transmitted to him, immediately upon the completion of each interrogation. By 1245 hours on Day 2, Rick had begun receiving and reading the reports.

He had been receiving after-action reports since the previous evening and knew that the invaders were in the range of 5000 to 6000 strong. He knew that it wasn't just superior manpower, weaponry and combat expertise that caused such a complete rout of the enemy. It was also their ignorance of key facts which spelled their doom. And almost every key fact was somehow connected to Rick's unit.

There was the exhaustive research which allowed the unit to build a model of HARP and identify its players; Clarissa's solo venture to Charleston; the revealing writing which came back with her; and Ben and Chris Berger's bugging of Spence's Citadel meeting were also important. Rick's recruitment of Clarissa to, in turn, recruit Deidre, who proved to be a spectacular undercover agent, was pivotal. Then there were the encoded messages Deidre passed on to Rick, by which they were able to identify San Francisco as the target. Another successful venture was the well-executed plan which neutralized Scherzer, Hajib, Q and Collins; and rendered Spence dysfunctional. It cut off the terrorists' only means of communication and intelligence.

Finally, the brilliant field work by Hirsch, Dubinsky and Agent 11932421 enabled them to obtain a detailed map of exactly where the hostiles were deployed. That coup d'état proved to be decisive.

Rick allowed himself to ruminate for a moment on the methodology by which they were able to achieve victory. Now Spence was the last double-sided man standing among their enemies. Rick's historical study of the methods of Elliott, Philby and Angleton paid a dividend he never expected. By mastering as much as he could of their paradigm—of the brilliant body of work they had done during World War II and the Cold War—he and Fasbender were able to pull off a resounding victory without subjecting a single enemy agent to torture. There had been no waterboarding, sleep deprivation, drugging, exposures to extremes of heat and cold, or tethering prisoners in painful positions.

Rick's view of those methods was that they were a product of laziness and moral laxity. A poor substitute for spending the time and energy to employ sound espionage and counterespionage tradecraft. A substitute born of laziness and brutality, not intellect and imagination. Such practices demeaned the United States.

The casualties so far: two agents killed, two others wounded; eight combat troops dead and nineteen wounded; twenty-five civilian casualties but only two fatalities. But enough basking in the sunshine of success! Things were far from over and the interrogation reports were beginning to pile up, unread.

Rick found a large closet with a desk and lamp, closed the door and began reading in earnest. By the time he finished he felt the pangs of hunger. He glanced at his watch as he headed for the cafeteria and was shocked to see that it was 1900 hours. He had been reading for six straight hours.

After devouring the meatloaf special, washed down with a Pepsi, Rick felt renewed and re-energized. He never forgot that no matter what fancy title he held, he was—like his father before him—an analyst above all else. And something in his analyst's soul was troubling him. Fortunately, he had highlighted in yellow those portions of the interrogation reports which he considered the most significant. He wouldn't have to read them through a second time in their entirety.

After a brief phone conversation with Clarissa, during which she expressed her elation that the crisis was over and Rick was safe, he returned to his isolation closet, locked the door and began rereading the highlighted sections of the reports.

This time he brought a small portable TV with him and switched it on to CNN so he could hear the President address the nation on its victory in San Francisco. The media were already well into their feeding frenzy, with one national network adopting as its lead-in the catch phrase, "Triumph in the Homeland, Jihad routed."

Rick was disgusted by this piece of Jingoism which suggested, absurdly, that the United States had decisively vanquished its foes.

Such vacuous prose was more than Rick could stand. He turned off the TV and vowed that it would stay off.

He decided that in his second phase of studying the interrogation reports, he would concentrate on those captured combatants in position of leadership. Somewhat arbitrarily he settled on those no lower in the pecking order than platoon leader. Over the next half hour he winnowed his list of unit leaders down to twenty, ranging from platoon leaders at the low end to battalion commanders at the top. Of the twenty captured officers, not a single one told anything about the details of their operations. But their interrogators were veteran CIA and FBI personnel who knew how to press the right buttons to get their subjects to open up a bit.

As an analyst, Rick had always relied on repetition to help him unearth deeper levels of meaning lying below the surface of a statement. In his current position as Chief of Counterintelligence he hammered home to his analysts the need to give him direct quotes from the subjects. He disliked paraphrasing and summaries. Unless there were some good excuse why not, he always wanted to know exactly what the subject was asked and what he answered.

War had seemed to shrink the world since 9/11 and many of the interrogators were now fluent in English and more than one Arabic dialect. On the other hand many of the prisoners knew English as well.

One frequently asked question was, "What was the objective of your operation?" Most gave canned answers, such as "to seek vengeance for Allah against the Infidel." But two of them gave the identical answer, carrying with it what seemed to be more strategically specific information: "Two cities." When pressed as to why, San Francisco and Oakland were selected, neither would answer. It seemed obvious to Rick that had it not been for the fact that Oakland was contiguous to San Francisco, it would have been an unlikely target—much the same as Denver, Albuquerque or Salt Lake City. Without San Francisco lying right across the Bay, Oakland would lack the cachet and headline potential of world-famous cities such as New York and San Francisco. But something was gnawing at Rick's brain. Something just didn't feel right. He decided he needed to reread the insurgents' pre-action and after-action reports, starting with those relating to Oakland; as well as the U.S. after-action reports.

After having a pot of coffee placed on the desk in his hideaway, Rick checked his watch and saw that it was now 2200 hours. He better call Clarissa and tell her he probably would be pulling another all-nighter. Since his small retreat had no landline, he was forced to use his cell phone.

The insurgents' reports were impressive in their detail. They identified launching points for multiple small units from various hidden locations in Marin County, with the largest unit on the coast of the Tiburon Peninsula. The landings in Oakland were to be made on crafts camouflaged as pleasure boats. The reports vividly described the manpower and weaponry on each craft, the intended points of arrival and the plans for coordination with the San Francisco insurgency.

The U.S. after-action reports included overhead photos of the Marin County units disbanding and withdrawing before launching could take place. The retreat occurred after they received word that the San Francisco infiltrators had been caught by surprise and routed.

Rick found nothing unusual in the retreat by the enemy but instinctively, he felt uneasy. He pulled out from a sizeable stack of captured enemy documents, the master operational plan. He moved

his index finger down the margin of the left side of the page—
translated into English by Army Intelligence—until he found the
entry, "Planned time of attack: 1430 hours; classification F.I.N."
F.I.N. was Army Intelligence code for "fully integrated.

In a nutshell, had U.S. and Canadian forces not attacked first, all
enemy units would have scrambled out of their rat holes to begin
their assault at 1430 hours, or 2:30 p.m. But presumably this also
included the units in Marin County whose objective was the City of
Oakland. Yet one did not need to be an expert in amphibious
operations to know that in order for those units to be in place at their
attack points in Oakland by 1430, they would have had to embark
from Marin no later than 1100 hours. Yet, here they were still on the
other side of the Bay at mid-afternoon. Something was really out of
whack. A hated word crept into Rick's consciousness. "Decoy." The
possible inference to be drawn was horrifying. When the captured
Jihadist officers referred to their objective as "two cities," one of the
two was San Francisco, but the other was probably not Oakland.

Rick sprang into action. He was back in his office in seconds and
on the intercom to Fasbender and Booker. "Gentlemen, come to my
office ASAP." He next emailed Deidre, which he had pledged to
himself to do only for extreme emergencies, and used their
prearranged code alphabet to order her to call him immediately. He
used a fresh iPhone which the Langley techs assured him could not
be traced. Deidre had now been off the grid for forty-eight hours.
Rick prayed that she would respond...that she was all right.

He called General Ortega directly on the secure line established
between them:

"Richmond, what's going on?"

"General, what's the status of the fleeing combatants from the
Tiburon Peninsula?"

"It's odd; we haven't been able to pick up much of a trail. We
caught about twenty of them in the Redwood Forest, another dozen
or so near the Sausalito coast but that's about it."

"Do you have any theory as to what happened to the rest of

them, General?"

"Nope, not a clue. We have picked up some suspicious cell phone traffic from the county seat, San Rafael, and I've dispatched a platoon of Delta troops to check it out. I'll let you know."

"Okay, thanks General."

Information corroborating one's worst fears is particularly chilling. Rick felt himself shudder as he signaled Booker and Fasbender into his office. The alleged Marin to Oakland phase of the enemy operation was looking more like a ruse all the time. The U.S. may have been duped into placing its forces in Oakland on high alert against a phantom, decoy, army. And as his father—his frequent mentor during his early years with the Company—always said to him, "A strongly assembled defense against a falsely perceived attack is almost always accompanied by a weak defense at the true point of attack."

Was Rick's mind playing games with him? Was he exaggerating the problem? He thought not, and anyway, there was—on the chance that he was right—no time to do anything but act.

Mort Fasbender and Doug Booker were rapidly briefed; the former registering surprise; the latter remaining stone-faced. Booker was never really surprised at anything because his supple mind unerringly weighed all the possibilities. This is what put him a cut above the rest.

"Think in polar opposites," said Booker. "If the expected Oakland attack was a decoy, don't expect an attack on Seattle or Los Angeles. Nor on Chicago or St. Louis. The real attack is likely to be at the polar opposite of the Bay Area. The Eastern Seaboard cities of Boston, New York, Philadelphia and Washington, were the most probable. The Jihadists' resources are probably stretched too thin to attack more than one of those cities. The question is, which of the four is the target?"

Fasbender was skeptical. He thought Booker spoke with an exaggerated sense of certitude. Rick had no doubt that Booker was right. After a quick phone call to Clarissa telling her to get out of

DC immediately and go inland as far as she could get, he again tried to reach Deidre, without success.

The three intelligence pros debated the issue of the where and when for the next half hour, without reaching even the most tentative consensus. The discussion did however, allow Rick to sift through his thoughts. "Only Spence and the top leadership of the Jihadists know, with the possible exception of Deidre." Fasbender and Booker nodded in silent agreement.

On a conference call among the three men in Rick's office with General Ortega and Ben Berger, Rick requested (actually ordered) that the most senior prisoners be pulled in and interrogated again, nonstop, for any information which might reveal the location of the next attack. Thus began the second major phase in one of America's largest counterinsurgency operations.

Events began to occur with breakneck speed. The President was informed and secretly ordered extensive new security measures in DC and environs: at national parks and monuments, government buildings, transportation facilities, the White House, Pentagon, CIA Headquarters, Congress, the Supreme Court and the FBI. The entire nation was placed on Red Alert.

The mayors of all major Eastern Seaboard cities, and the governors of their states, were personally warned as well. All national airports, train stations and harbors were brought into the loop, together with the directors of the FBI, CIA, ATF, DIA, NSA, Homeland Security and the Director of National Intelligence.

Rick added his father to the group within his office. The four of them began sifting through intelligence data while they conducted a free-form discussion among themselves—all directed at the key questions of the where, when and how of the probable next attack.

The President called Booker and Rick to an emergency national defense meeting at the White House. Booker left for the meeting after first convincing the President that Rick would be more valuable right where he was.

Booker's judgment was vindicated when Rick's iPhone alerted

him to a new text message. In his nervousness, he bungled the touch-sensitive access for "messages" twice, before it popped up on the screen of his phone.

It was from Deidre. He tried to contain his excitement as he opened the message. But, upon reading it, excitement morphed into alarm. Deidre had failed to encode the message. There it was, a harbinger of dread and horror. It consisted of only twelve words and fifty-four letters, but it might as well have been a multipage manifesto of doom.

"DC penetrated. Weaponized anthrax will go into HVAC vents on S's signal."

Rick's shock was so extreme he didn't later remember handing his cellphone to Fasbender and then to Tom Tallifierro, or how they reacted. The next thing he remembered was calling the President and reading the message to him. Of that conversation, he recalled the President saying only, "Stand down, we'll take it from here."

Stand-down? How could he stand-down? Who other than he had a chance of finding Spence and stopping him? To avoid a disaster of incalculable proportions he must act swiftly, even if it meant disobeying a presidential order.

Rick quickly responded to Deidre's message with a text message of his own:

"Where are you and what are the targets?"

It seemed to him an eternity before Deidre answered. It was actually only 40 seconds:

"Falls Church, Marriott, Rm. 19. S./sleeping. U have 20 min. at most. All buildings on or near mall targets."

Rick's hands shook as he pressed the intercom button for "Heliport."

"Special Agent Barnes speaking."

"Barnes this is Tallifierro. Have a chopper on the roof and ready to go in five minutes."

Rick steadied himself enough to strap on his shoulder holster. His Glock was in its place and fully loaded. He signaled to

Fasbender to do the same.

It took them seven minutes to reach the helipad located on the roof of the adjoining building in the Langley complex. Another three minutes passed before they were strapped in and the chopper lifted off.

"Where to sir?"

"Falls Church Marriott. Land on the roof and make it fast. This is a Defcon 2 emergency."

"Copy that."

Five minutes later the Black Hawk circled the Marriott.

"We can't land Sir. There's not enough room on the roof."

"Okay get as low as you can and drop a rope."

"It's still going to be a ten-foot drop, Sir."

"Just do it, now!"

Rick and Mort shimmied down the rope—Rick first. The drop to the roof was actually about 15 feet. Rick hit the asphalt surface feet-first. Flames shot through his ankles, his nerve endings transmitting the pain. Wing tips were not the ideal footwear for a fifteen-foot jump. But he didn't think he broke anything and Mort seemed okay too. Providence seemed to smile on them when they found the roof door unlocked. But Rick's quick gaze at his watch as they tore down the stairs caused his spirits to plunge. It was now nineteen minutes since he had received Deidre's text message. He prayed mightily that it would not be too late.

The two agents took three and sometimes four steps at a time as they raced down the five flights of stairs, with a landing between each floor. Their destination was the first floor and room 19. Each time their feet landed spasms of pain knifed through their ankles, which were undoubtedly sprained from the drop to the roof. Exactly 20 minutes after Deidre's message they reached the ground floor. Maybe they would still stop Spence from launching the attack. But their hopes were at least temporarily dashed when the exit door from the stairwell to first floor hallway was locked.

Fasbender quickly searched the stairwell and found an unhinged door lying underneath the stairs. The door was heavy and suitable as a battering ram. They picked up the door, held it face-side up and with all the force they could muster, charged the locked door and rammed it. Their bodies, spiked with adrenalin, managed to loosen the door on its hinges but not break through it. A second try seemed to loosen it more but it still held. They were now two full minutes beyond the allotted time.

Were they to be thwarted in their attempt to save thousands of innocent lives by the pure obstinacy of a locked door? "Not acceptable!" bellowed Rick. Fasbender got the message.

The two men gathered themselves anew and charged the door with the fury of a wounded rhinoceros. The improvised battering ram smashed into the door with a force few wooden structures could withstand. Chunks of wood and jagged pieces of metal flew into the hallway. The previously obdurate barrier crashed to the floor. Fortunately, no one was unlucky enough to be in the door's path when it gave, or in the zone of flying splinters, chunks of sharp wood and metal.

They were in but not yet there. They emerged from the stairwell in front of room 1. Room 19 was a good three hundred feet further down the long corridor. As they turned and raced down the hall, distant shouting was followed by the explosion of a gunshot. Rick instantly feared for Deidre's life. The agents picked up their pace, sprained ankles notwithstanding. They drew their weapons at about twenty feet before reaching Room 19. A second later Deidre emerged from a room in a state of hysteria, oblivious to their presence. She opened the unlocked door to room 20 directly opposite number 19 and entered. The sounds of her screams pierced the quiet of the hallway. Fasbender pressed his body against the left wall, Rick against the right, as they moved forward with weapons held in the firing position. Fasbender quickly looked into Room 20; and Rick did the same as to Room 19. Both shouted "freeze" as they entered. Mort Fasbender found Deidre lying face down on her bed, muttering the same words over and over between sobs, "I stopped him; I stopped him." Rick dashed into Room 19 ready for a shoot out. Instead he found Spence lying face down on his bed with a jagged and bleeding gunshot hole in the back of his head.

Chapter Eighteen

THE FINAL RECKONING

The County Prosecutor made a decision within twenty-four hours after Deidre killed her father that not only was it justifiable homicide but she ought to get a medal for her actions. By her solitary, courageous act, she had prevented Spence from giving the attack signal. Had the attack occurred, it probably would have been the worst single incident of biological warfare in history. The White House was considering awarding to Deidre the Presidential Medal of Freedom. The smart money was on an affirmative decision and a quick one.

The Jihadists had hated Spence but they were a wily bunch and respected his unique knowledge and access. They knew that without a go-ahead from Spence, the attack was not likely to succeed. So, when no signal was given at the appointed time, they aborted the attack and most promptly scurried towards the Potomac bridges to escape to Virginia. Some headed for the Maryland border.

The White House had spurred Acting FBI Director, Clyde Underwood into action. Underwood sealed the land border and the bridges so tightly that only a few terrorists were able to escape from the District of Columbia. Skirmishes between the two hundred and fifty Jihadists on one side and the National Guard, FBI, DC Police, Navy Seals and Army Rangers on the other, lasted for five days. When it was over 175 Jihadists had either been killed by American forces and police or committed suicide. A few died from anthrax poisoning and over sixty were taken prisoner. The prisoners were first interrogated and then shipped off to Guantanamo.

The criminal trials in Federal District Court for the District of Columbia of Foster Wright a.k.a. "Q," Mark Scherzer, Henry Hajib and Kyle Collins dragged on for two years. Their appeals took another two. When all the dust finally settled, "Q" and Collins were sentenced to life and sent to Leavenworth federal penitentiary. Hajib got thirty years and Scherzer twenty-five.

Deidre and Clarissa fully reconciled and the latter named her first born daughter after her now-famous sister. Deidre Tallifierro was followed in the line of succession by the birth of Douglas, Thomas II and Clarissa. There was no doubt after whom the four Tallifierro children were named.

The private investigation agency founded by Ben and Chris Berger and bolstered by the fame gathered from the "Attacks on Two Cities," grew over a two-year period from three employees to two hundred and twenty-seven, comprised by investigators, computer programmers, security guards, drone operators, polygraphers, and clerical staff.

The two person teams created by Rick were incorporated into the CIA's Counterintelligence Branch. All the team members with the exception of Torres were hired as full-time employees. Their new boss was the Chief of Counterintelligence, Morton Fasbender. They bore the new name, "The Critical Response Unit." Cynthia Torres returned to the U.S. Attorney's office to head the antiterrorism task force.

Rick was appointed Deputy Director of the CIA on his 38th birthday. Twenty-eight months later at the age of forty, Richmond

Tallifierro became the youngest Director of the C.I.A. in history.

Islamic Jihad continued. Organizations like ISIS, al Qaeda and Boca Haram continued to spread death and destruction in the U.S.A., Great Britain, Continental Europe, the Middle East, the Far East and Africa. But they also suffered as many defeats as victories. The successful defense of the two cities became a textbook model for defeating terrorism on one's home soil.

A relatively small group of intelligence analysts and agents had, by dint of their wits, bravery and love of country, helped the U.S. decisively repel the attacks on the "two cities" without sustaining major casualties. And no matter what battles lay ahead, this was an accomplishment no one could take away from them.

Chris Berger wrote a four hundred and fifty-page book on Jihadism in America, post 9/11. It was entitled "At War with the Fanatical Foe." Its theme was that in the war against Islamic terrorism there was no clear winner. Although he lauded the Bush and Obama administrations for their skill and determination in combating al Qaeda and ISIS, particularly in decimating the infrastructure of al Qaeda, he strongly criticized the many oversights, blunders and failures of execution in both American and European counterterrorism efforts.

Berger identified the main culprit as the lack of perseverance and focus by both citizens and leaders in consistently seeing Jihadism for what it is. Most had simply not come to terms with the existential threat it posed to the world. At many important junctures after 9/11, wrote Berger, "Western populaces and their leaders have allowed themselves to lapse into complacency and inattention." Contributing causes to the languor and malaise are the 72-hour news cycle, the polarization of the U.S.'s two major political parties, the penetrating glare of the 24/7 cable news media and the attention deficit syndrome everywhere, which seemed to be growing to pandemic proportions, abetted by the social media.

Berger's book was as insightful as it was informative: a wakeup call to the world to abandon its self-destructive attitudes and habits.

Interviews with former CIA directors, George Tenet and Leon Panetta, manifested an unanimity between them that a shocking percentage of Americans didn't even realize that we have been "at war" since bin Laden declared it against us in 1996, twenty years ago. In 1998 the CIA learned that bin Laden had met with Pakistani officials and asked for their help in making a nuclear bomb.

Berger deplored the lack of communication among the government agencies charged with our safety. An FBI agent in an office in the southwestern United States was unable in the months leading up to 9/11 to get her supervisor in Washington to take seriously her report that Middle Eastern men—believed to be Muslims—were receiving lessons on how to take off and fly large passenger airliners, but were skipping the lessons on how to land them.

And personnel of the CIA knew that three known al Qaeda members were on the passenger manifest of one of the airliners which crashed into the World Trade Towers, but neglected to share the information with the FBI, or even with the higher-ups in the CIA.

*   *   *

Deidre Wilson required ongoing psychotherapy to cope with her guilt over killing her father. At government expense she received regular treatment at Johns Hopkins Medical Center in Baltimore, where she was reported to be making progress. Clarissa accompanied Deidre to her sessions whenever she was able to find the time. The entire Spence family suffered psychological trauma from learning just who Paul Spence really was, but were working hard, with the aid of professionals, to cope with the circumstances of his death and the notoriety which quickly followed.

As to the often turbulent relationship between Rick and Clarissa, both would admit that although they never outwardly acknowledged it, Paul Spence had been a great weight on their marriage. With the wisdom of hindsight they saw fully how devious and insidious were his methods. Through guile and exploiting his genetic connection, he malevolently sought to recruit Clarissa to his cause and plant the seeds of suspicion in her relationship with Rick. Years of psychological abuse during her childhood and adolescence had made her vulnerable. But ultimately, the strong and independent person she had become won out. The same could be said of Deidre except that in her case both the conversion and the ultimate rehabilitation were far more radical and traumatic.

In their new partnership, Tallifierro and Fasbender sought to learn from both the successes and failures of America's counterterrorism program. Thwarted Muslim extremist conspiracies to bomb the bridges and tunnels of New York City and to plant bombs on wide-body airliners headed from various points in Europe to America, were examples of great successes by the U.S. intelligence community. The Boston Marathon bombing and the San Bernardino shootings were among their greatest failures. They were acutely aware that homegrown terrorists posed a monumental threat to the homeland. They were an evil entity unto themselves, requiring ever-vigilant attention.

Subtly the "War on Terrorism" was becoming more streamlined, better coordinated and better balanced between domestic and foreign threats. The number of undercover agents had reached a new zenith and was proving to be very effective. And to Rick's great credit, traditional espionage tradecraft in both intelligence and counterintelligence operations was enjoying a renaissance.

After Douglas Booker finally sat down on his Virginia farm to write his memoirs, the lessons learned from the assault upon the two cities were highlighted in a stirring final chapter. The final chapter in the war against terrorism was yet to be written.

Other Books By Donald J. Farinacci

THE SPY WARS TRILOGY

A friendship formed in World War II may be the only thing that can stop World War III...

ISBN: 978-0-983416-81-4

The world's nuclear superpowers are rushing toward what may be their final confrontation. The countdown to Armageddon is on...

ISBN: 978-0-985252-35-9

NONFICTION

The story of the political battle between President Dwight D. Eisenhower and Senator Joseph McCarthy for the moral leadership of the nation.

ISBN: 978-1-499780-85-7

The story of U.S. District Court Judge John J. Sirica's courageous battle to defeat the criminal conspiracy led by President Richard M. Nixon.

ISBN: 978-1-438977-82-9

A tribute to those who actually fought the Vietnam War and became collateral victims of a wrenching cultural war, not of their own making.

ISBN: 978-1-434318-57-2

The story of two extraordinary men, President Harry S. Truman and General Douglas MacArthur, and the collision of wills that changed American history.

ISBN: 978-0557409-02-0